Vaguely, George wondered where he was supposed to be that day. An office, a factory, perhaps? Certainly not here in Central Park. Who was he, he wondered? But then he looked at Lynn, her blonde hair framed partly by the bright greens of the Park and partly by the bright blues of the Manhattan sky above the irregular shapes of the Central Park West towers, and he didn't care.

MAXWELL E. SIEGEL was born in Brooklyn and has traveled widely. But his first love is Manhattan Island, where his lyrics have been sung and his plays produced—off-off-Broadway. There he has worked in a nine-to-five job and then enjoyed the open spaces of Central Park. Mr. Siegel and his wife now live in the even wider spaces of a New Jersey farm.

THE LAUREL-LEAF LIBRARY ngs together under a si ks of fiction and for young adult classroom. The se Charles F. Reason Education, New Y

D1355277

Central Park Underground

Max Siegel

Published by
Dell Publishing Co., Inc.
1 Dag Hammarskjold Plaza
New York, New York 10017

Laurel-Leaf Library ® TM 766734,
Dell Publishing Co., Inc.

ISBN: 0-440-91168-0

Reprinted by arrangement with Walker and Company.
Printed in the United States of America
First Laurel-Leaf printing—April 1977
Second Laurel-Leaf printing—October 1977

For Georgette

All persons and places in this story are fictitious. Central Park is purely a product of the author's imagination; New York City, a state of his mind.

Contents

Prologue

In Central Park after midnight, strange shapes and shadows can be seen by the brave, combining and recombining into inexhaustible permutations of frightening silhouettes under the feeble light of the converted gas lamps. Soft whistles are answered in a kind of code. Strange rustlings can be heard in trash cans and behind privets. A soft, heavy blanket of hot summer blackness can turn a child's laugh into the semblance of a vulture's shrill cry. Padded, prowling footsteps echo unseen through acres of emptiness. At night the Park becomes a vast sea of apprehension surrounded by a thin border of giggles and heavy breathing.

Near the western edge of the Park, Belvedere Tower, with its haunted Gothic parapets, stands like a sentinel over the deserted pond and baseball diamonds below. And on the patch leading up the cliff to the Tower, a strange shadow play was taking place.

The outline of a man, carved by a white August moon, skimmed along the patch and off onto the black grass, where it became motionless. Slowly, another shadow became visible, moving up behind the first; one arm was raised above its head and terminated in an ominously dangling blob. The second shadow advanced on the first until they were about to merge; then, the blob came down. The first shadow staggered back.

"For Christ's sake, Herman," a hoarse whisper grated through the night. "You nearly hit me that time."

"Sorry, George. But did I get it right this time?"

"No, you numbskull. First of all, I could hear those

Number Elevens of yours clumping fifty feet away. And then I smelled your breath at least half a minute before you were set to bop. How many times have I told you to hold your breath and to come up fast?"

"That's right, George."

"I know it's right. And I think it's a waste of time to try to teach you anything."

"Ah, no, George. I'll get it. Honest I will. Look, this time you mug me, and I'll watch you do it right. OK?"

The first shadow threw up its hands, and as it moved into a hazy circle of light, turned into a medium-sized, husky, knobby man who could have been anything from a masseur to a subway guard. His companion, who was carrying a rather limp-looking blackjack, was similarly built. The two of them together looked like a pair of bookends for the collected works of Damon Runyon.

"All right, George," said the one named Herman Krugwerksch, "I'll be the mark this time. Here's the cosh."

"The what?"

"The cosh, ain't that right? I heard it once on TV."

"Cosh," George Castello mumbled, more to himself and his gods than to Herman. "Cosh, for Christ's sake."

"Just give me an even chance, George. I bet I could do it pretty good now. All I have to do is see it once more."

"OK," said Castello. "Give me the blackjack. You just stand there for a while."

He took the truncheon from Herman's moist hands and faded away into the blackness. Herman strained his eyes to see into the shadows, but he could not make out anything beyond the comparatively bright ellipse of light in which he was standing.

"George?" Herman whispered the name as if it would lighten the dark and help him see his friend. "George, where are you?"

There was no answer. Herman looked nervously around him for a moment and then moved off into the darkness of the path. "George?" Suddenly he heard a rustling noise to his right. He whirled around, but saw nothing except the branch of a tree trembling against the sky.

"George?"

A nervous perspiration began to bead on his forehead. If there was one thing Herman did not like, it was to be alone in Central Park without George.

"George? George, come back."

The night at once seemed full of strange whooshings and scrapings. An ardent nature-lover could have pointed out several of academic interest: a gray squirrel (*Sciuridae carolinensis*) gnawing off the soft top of a premature green acorn; a song sparrow (*Melospiza melodia*) brightly inquiring of no one in particular if he might satisfy a mysterious mating urge; the surly scurrying of a big rat (*Rattus*) trying to make his way back to the nice cool basement of a tenement for the night. Not only did Herman not appreciate this zoological display, but he was becoming rapidly convinced that the noises were getting louder and closer.

"George?"

He took a step back, and then leaped around with a strangled shriek as he felt a hand on his shoulder. It was Castello.

"You look nervous," he said, not unkindly. "Is anything the matter?"

"I want out of here right this minute, George. I'm scared. This place is unnatural—how do I know what might be going on around here? Let's get out."

Castello sighed deeply. "OK, Herman. I guess it's back to Times Square and dipping. But we coulda had it soft here. I—"

He broke off.

Just down the path, under a remote yellow splash from a distant lamp, he could see the approaching figure of a lone pedestrian.

"Tell ya what, Herman. Just stand here and shut up. Let me knock this one over, and then we'll scram. Right?"

"You won't leave me alone too long, will ya, George?"

"Naw. Just stand where you are, and give me a few minutes."

Castello disappeared into the dark again and Herman sat down by the side of the path. In the distance he could see the solitary walker move through another patch of illumination on his way up the path. Herman tried humming to himself for a while and then began digging aimlessly in the grass, scratching out pebbles and flicking them down the hill.

One rock seemed to be giving him some trouble; he placed his hand flat on the ground behind him to get more leverage. That is, he intended to place it on the ground, but instead he placed in on *Rattus*, who had just polished off one mysterious meal and was starting on another, even clammier. The effect on both of them was about the same. The rat dropped his prize and, in one fearful bound, made his way breathlessly to a crevice in the rocky cliff that dropped down to the water below.

Herman had left his rock-climbing days behind him many years ago, but he was as true to his reflex as the rat had been to his. He bolted upright, as if a white-hot iron had been applied to his coccyx, and screamed, "George!"

Just at that moment he saw the pedestrian, who had reached the next lamplit area, stop short and begin to look around. Herman broke off a second "Geo—" as he saw his partner's figure bound up from the shrubbery and bring his blackjack down on his victim's head. The man crumpled and Castello pushed him quickly out of the light.

Herman loped down the path, his hand still tingling from the nameless horror with which it had been in contact. "I don't care if George is mad. I gotta get out of here," he was saying to himself.

1 How a Voice Told Fortunes and the Lights Went Out

The young man was miserable. A dwarf with a heavy sledge was engaged in driving a railroad spike through his cranium, from the inside, at a point roughly midway between his right ear and the back of his head. To make matters somewhat more engaging, his mouth felt as if it had been used as a latrine by a number of small woolly animals who had only recently vacated the premises.

When he reached up cautiously to explore the damage, he was simultaneously relieved and puzzled. Relieved, because he found that all of his vital protuberances and apertures were still situated in approximately the correct relation to one another and that the main connections to his body were still in good shape. Puzzled, because the top of his head was wrapped in what seemed to be a turban composed of innumerable yards of white muslin, pieces of which hung down on all sides in a Medusa-like permanent.

These facts became apparent to him only over a longish time interval. Curiously enough, his first thoughts upon awakening were on the order of "Where am I?" Now, it is well known that any person who receives a painful rap on the edge of the occiput, administered in anything more than friendly exasperation, will immediately upon coming into consciousness exclaim, "Where am I?" It is a valuable straight line, as well as an inviting come-on to the exposition, where a slinky Oriental, dressed in an Adrain sarong left over from *Moon Over Tahumakami*, ripostes, "You are in the grand chamber of the imposing master, presumptuous white man, for having dared to meddle in the affair of the sacred *fella-hin*." The young man retained some measure of originality by not really saying, "Where am I?" out loud. He wasn't ashamed, but he was not at all certain of his vocal cords, or of any other part of his anatomy as yet. True to form, however, he followed this novel thought with another no less original. "*Who am I?*"

In his favor, it should be remarked that he did not frame either idea in exactly those words. He awoke with a lingering feeling of not existing, a feeling that lasted for an alarming amount of time. A vague sense of loss, of emptiness, was fastened tightly onto his mind, as if something important—the Empire State Building, say—was suddenly missing and the loss could not quite be identified. Since everyone knows that people do not suffer amnesia when they are hit over the head, except in comic novels and Marx Brothers movies, let us say that the young man was bewildered.

He will remain bewildered for about eight days.

While the young man was busy dwelling uncertainly on his situation, a Voice was gradually impressing itself on his consciousness. This voice was enough to give a lesser man the heebie-jeebies, or even an equivalent man in full possession of his perception. To this young man, the Voice was simply that—a Voice. And it was saying, in trembling, highly inflected, spooky tones, something like:

". . . very sure. Yes, very sure that something quite terrible is hanging over all of us. All of our fates are bound together like . . . Yes, here it is! We are one, and it is . . . It is . . . No, I shouldn't have looked. You should never have come. I am seeing myself through your . . . through your . . . through your what, for God's sake? Through your hand? Nuts. Through your . . . in the mirror of your destiny. That's neat. OK, that's for getting rid of deadbeats. Now, some thoughts on business types between lunch and five o'clock. Type one: three to five martinis or equivalent. I see a man. A strong man. His vibrations are incredibly strong through your eyes. He is an evil man. I see him controlling you. No! It is not possible! I see you as a puppet, and this man is pulling the strings. That's pretty good. You are unhappy—you are trying to pull back, but this evil man is hurting you. OK, he says it's his boss, and gives the trampling on initiative bit, et cetera, et cetera. Please! You must try to think of something else. This picture is drowning out all vibrations. Oh, damn. There are those finky vibrations again. There must be something better. Let's see. This is the twentieth century, and if I can't do better than vibrations, I might as well . . . There we go. Psychonics. Psychonic waves! Mercedes Gitana, you may have a bestseller on your hands. Psychonic waves. My, my. So, OK, you schlub, your stupid boss is drowning out all the psychonics. Where do we go from here? I see a small house . . . a low house . . . a tree . . ."

The young man was not sure enough of the Voice's place in his new scheme of things to make any kind of judgment on his monologue. It appeared to alternate between a reverent, bloodcurdling moan and a crisp matter-of-factness—between spirits (incorporeal) and spirits (high). It was all the more puzzling in that the Voice did not appear to be addressing anyone, least of all himself. It simply arrived, alone, from an area of light too far behind him for him to see what it was all about without risking the detachment of his spine. For a while, therefore, he thought it would be advisable to lie still and hurt, while the Voice droned inexorably on.

". . . your late husband. Some trouble is brewing— I can't put my finger on it. What is that? Yes, I feel it now. A cold wind is speaking your name, whatever it is. Too hokey. More scientific direction. Something like, the thoughts are assembling. There is much disturbance in the signal—in the waves—as if there is a reluctance to be known. Ask why and find out all about the problem. Good. Everything is clearer now. He is saying blah-blah-blah and forgives you. Still pretty hokey, but better. Now for a college type. Oh, so you're back among the living. Don't try to get up. I'll be right there."

This last was spoken in neither the spooky nor the matter-of-fact tone, but in a surprisingly cheerful voice, overlaid with a certain measure of concern. The young man realized, with a start, that it was probably directed at him; he braced himself for a view of the Voice when it moved into his restricted optical range. He was not disappointed.

The Voice was a tall, reasonably attractive woman somewhere in what has been called perpetual middle age. She was dressed informally in an old sweatshirt and a pair of mauve toreador pants, and managed to resemble nothing quite so much as Peter Pan subject to the normal laws of time and nature. Her smile was warming, but when the young man tried to return it, he felt as if the corners of his mouth were cutting through a series of taut tendons. He stopped the gesture, hurriedly.

"Are you all right?" the Voice said worriedly. "If not, just shake your head—only if you can, that is," she added as he tried to do something, and just as quickly, with a grimace, gave up. "Just wave your hand, and I'll call an ambulance or something. Freddy and I found you on the path near the stairs; neither of us particularly wanted to call a cop if it wasn't completely necessary. And since we didn't know how long it would be until you were found, I thought we should bring you here for a while at least. Do you think you'll—well— get better?"

"I just feel a little woozy," the young man said, startling both of them, "but I think I'll make it."

"Goodness," said the Voice, "you can talk. That's a relief. I was afraid for a moment we might have to see about getting some help. Freddy said you'd be out for a good half a day, with no permanent damage. It's hard to believe, but I guess he was right. He's had more experience with these things than I have."

"Half a day?" The idea floated in and out of the

young man's consciousness like an incredible fantasy. "What time is it?"

The Voice looked at her wristwatch. "Four-fifteen, Wednesday afternoon. I make it about fourteen or fifteen hours that you've been out, allowing an hour or so before we found you.'

The idea of being unconscious for so long fascinated the young man. Besides, he was slowly delighting in finding himself more or less in one workable piece, and he began to experiment with sitting up.

"I hope I don't have him to thank for this head."

"Who, Freddy? You mean, for the *mugging?* Oh, Lord, no," exclaimed the Voice. "Freddy wanted to call for help right away but I suggested we try to wait for a while, as long as it didn't look particularly serious. Do you want a drink?"

The young man's head was a little easier to shake at this point, so he shook it. "Give me a few more minutes. I must have had a nasty shot."

"It did look rather frightening, but Freddy said they all look like that at first. Let's take a look."

As she leaned over to unwrap the turban, the young man felt oddly relaxed, as if he had returned to some unknown past and his mother (surely he had, or had had, a mother) was exploring the aftereffects of a schoolyard disagreement.

The Voice was uncertain. "It still doesn't look too awfully good. Perhaps if I touch it—Does this hurt? Oh, I guess it did. I'm sorry. I suppose we ought to cover it up for a while longer. Some ice, I think, will do just fine."

The ice did just fine and the young man felt particularly grateful as the turban was being rewound.

"Thank you, Voice," he said.

"What?"

"Voice. I've somehow come to think of you as Voice. It fits you."

She laughed—a rather interesting, deep-toned, satisfying laugh. "Call me Sally."

"Sally."

"Aren't you going to say 'Where am I?' or 'Who am I?' or something like that?"

The young man winced. "As a matter of fact. I was planning to ask both questions but I was hoping that the answers would come out in the conversation. However, let's go. Where am I?"

Sally hesitated for a moment. "I'd really prefer not to tell you just yet. Let's say you're in my apartment."

The young man looked around. His vision had improved considerably in the previous fifteen minutes, but the dimness of the lighting still made it difficult to see clearly. The place appeared to be cavernous. The wall next to his cot was of rough-cut stone; the floor was concrete. A few small rugs were scattered around. Behind him, a bright area under a hanging reflector contained an old desk, a chair, and a tape recorder. He pegged this arrangement as explaining something about the Voice.

"It's a rather interesting apartment."

"For the record," said Sally, "we can call it a basement apartment."

"Near the Park?"

She hesitated again. "You could say that."

By this time the young man was sitting upright on the edge of the cot and Sally the Voice was sitting just opposite him on a chair. Looking at her more closely, he was even more favorably impressed. She had blue eyes, bright enough to be apparent at a distance of a few feet, and short light brown hair hanging in rather ragged bangs halfway down her forehead. Her features were carved with that heavy-handed fineness that is the first sign of approaching age, with a little-girl nose throwing the entire composition into the confusing realm of high art. A few gray hairs and a certain setness in the lines around her mouth and chin were the only other signs that would put her age late in the forties rather than five or ten years earlier. And her voice, in conversation, was soft, low, and had a trace of a smoothness not too common in midtown New York.

"Where are you from?"

"That's the wrong question. You're supposed to ask next 'Who am I?' "

"That's what I asked. Who are you?"

She laughed another satisfying laugh.

"Will you go back to the script if I tell you where I'm from?"

"Yes."

"Alabama."

That explained that, he thought. "Who am I?"

Sally laughed again, but this one was not quite as satisfying as the last two.

"You're kidding."

"No. Honestly, I seem to be a little vague about what I'm doing here, or who I am, or anything not particularly having to do with you or getting clobbered last night—it was last night, wasn't it?"

"This morning, actually. But this is awful. If you can't remember who you are, you must be in terrible danger."

"I feel fine," said the young man. "It's really very curious. I feel as if I had just awakened in a strange bed—you know, the overnight-trip, new-hotel feeling— except that the first moment of awakening is stretching out. I'm sure it will come back to me any minute now, so don't worry about it. I seem to be OK, otherwise."

Sally shook her head, "Maybe I'd better call the cops, anyway. They could probably find out who you are."

The young man stood up, but decided it was a bad idea when the room began to tilt crazily around him. Sitting down hurriedly, he said, "How about my wallet? That should—"

Sally interrupted almost as soon as his hand had gone to his hip pocket and felt it empty. "They must have taken everything. All you had was a handkerchief and a couple of theater stubs."

He brightened. "Maybe . . . I guess not." He un-brightened. It did not seem to be feasible to trace two theater seats to any particular identity.

"We found these keys near you on the path. Are they yours?"

He looked at the three keys on the ring she was holding up. Other than the fact that one was smaller than the others and looked like the key to a drawer or small box, there was nothing about them that hit him particularly. "Anything written on them?"

" 'Yale' on the two big ones. Is that your name?"

The young man felt that the coincidence would be too great. "I don't really think so. The odds are pretty heavily against it."

"I suppose you're right," said Sally. "How about your first name? Can you remember that?"

He had been trying to answer that question since he had awakened. Nothing sounded quite right, although he felt a familiar name buzzing in the back of his consciousness. He had been trying to trap it for almost a half-hour, but somehow it had remained elusive.

"Suppose I try some on you, for size."

"Try away," he said. He seemed to feel it had one syllable and started with an "R."

"Ralph," she said.

"No," he answered, startled.

"Frank."

"No."

"Harry."

"Uh-uh."

"Ummm. Richard—Dick."

"Nope."

"John."

"George," he said.

The name "George" had been the annoying thought flitting about in the recesses of his memory; somehow he had managed to bring it down with one well-placed shot as it flew fleetingly into range. *George.* He could remember a voice shouting at him, he could remember that name, and he could remember only that.

"It's funny," the young man said. "I don't feel as if I'm an absolute blank. Nothing that melodramatic at all. I seem to be in pretty good shape—I have all sorts of memories and bits of information floating around. I just can't seem to fasten onto anything that belongs to me personally. Now, for instance, the name 'George.' It feels very right, and yet somehow I'm not really sure it's mine. I just believe it means something to me." Suddenly he was frightened. Sally must have sensed his mood, because she tried to laugh it off.

"We're making progress, anyway," she said brightly. "George you are then, for the duration. I bet you'll catch up with that identity in jig time. But for now, how about that drink in celebration of your lost Wednesday?"

"Fine," said the newly christened George.

"What would you like?"

"Scotch and water." It slipped out before he could really think about it. Another useless clue.

Sally disappeared into another part of the room. A light clicked on and the young man could see a fairly well-equipped kitchen standing in a corner that had rock walls like the ones near him. It looked comfortable enough, but rather strange . . . strange . . . strange . . .

He felt very sleepy all at once, as if he had already had the drink. He stretched, murmured "George" to himself a few times, then fell into a deep and dreamless sleep.

When he awoke for the second time, the Voice was droning on as if nothing had happened. As a matter of fact, George thought for a moment that nothing had, for the words were startlingly familiar.

". . . et cetera. Please! You must try to think of something else. This picture is drowning out all the vibrations. Oh, damn. There are those finky vibrations again. There must be something better. Let's see. This is the twentieth century, and if I can't do better than vibrations I might as well . . ."

However, it was not exactly a matter of having heard all of it before, since a new sound had been added: the erratic clattering of a typewriter. George felt reasonably well enough constructed and buttressed to turn over on his side and take a peek in the direction of the sound.

At the table sat a very pretty young girl, typing expertly on a sleek foreign portable while Sally's gibberish droned from the tape recorder. George inspected this new addition to the ménage as well as he was able, considering the distance and the angle between them.

From the rear three-quarter view he had, she appeared to be the prototype of the Hollywood college coed, busily cramming for a term paper. She wore a man's white shirt, rolled up at the sleeves, and a pair of faded Levis that had certainly seen better days, though probably not better contents. She was bent low over the typewriter, and a wisp of her blond hair fell forward nearly to the platen. It was obviously a stray wisp, because most of her hair was banded into a short pony tail that ended somewhere in the vicinity of her shoulderblades. Her profile, which stood out sharply against the overhead light, was as regular as a director could have wished: her forehead was wide, her eyelashes long, her nose just a bit snubbed, as Sally's had been, and her chin was inconspicuously pointed. At this particular moment the only jarring note was provided by her lips, which were pursed in heavy concentration over her typing.

Sally was nowhere to be seen.

George switched to his elbows and rested his head on his open hands. He watched the girl scrupulously taking down the monologue and wondered how old she was. In spite of the general teen-age effect, he pegged her as being more advanced along in the twenties—there was something about the Levis, and the shirt to which her pointed chin kept distractingly pointing, that kept telegraphing messages to George which far exceeded the fifteen-word limit. He was also looking at a very nice ankle that protruded from the denim where her left leg, on which she was sitting, stuck out from under her right thigh, on which she was not, when Sally's voice broke through his funk.

"Oh, so you're back among the living. Don't try to get up. I'll be right there."

The girl jumped up, startled, and stared at George. George, a bit shaken himself realized that this last bit merely signaled the end of the tape Sally had been recording when he had regained consciousness the first time. They stared at each other mutely for a moment, while the recorder slowly transferred about thirty-five inches of tape from one reel to another. Then the girl laughed—a quick outbreath followed by a chuckle that ascended the scale until it became a squeal, which she promptly hid behind her hand. Then it was George's turn, and soon the both of them were roaring together, while the recorder began joining the conversation again.

"Dangerous . . . dangerous," it was saying hollowly. "You must leap in the face of opportunity, but you must have good footing. Goddamn! That sounds like a fortune cookie."

George and the girl broke up in peals of laughter again, and the girl switched off the machine.

"It did sound rather like a fortune cookie," she said. "Mother's right."

George did not say "Aha!" but he would have if he had thought of it.

"Sally is your mother?"

"You've met her? Oh, you must have gone back to sleep. She was gone when I came back, and I started in to transcribe the routine. By the way, how are you?"

George wasn't sure, but he took stock.

"Fine."

"Good. You were looking pretty chintzy when Mother and Freddy brought you in, but Freddy said you'd recover."

"So your mother told me. I'm glad that Freddy had

such great confidence in my recuperative powers. Actually, I was in doubt myself, for a while there."

"Well, I'm glad we're not going to have to call the police. After all, you've been out for an awfully long time."

"What time is it?" asked George.

"Five," said the girl unhelpfully.

"That's funny, I thought I was conked out for longer than an hour," George said. "The V—I mean, your mother said it was four the last time I rejoined the living."

The girl was looking at him oddly. "Four o'clock—when?"

An invisible finger ran up and down George's vertebrae. "Isn't it still Wednesday afternoon?"

"Well, actually—no. It's Thursday morning. You've had quite a snooze."

George was startled. "Good God. It really was a lost Wednesday. I haven't been out that long since—" He hesitated blankly. "Well, since."

The girl seemed suddenly solicitous again. "Are you sure you feel well enough to get up? We can help you back home when it's daylight."

George keenly felt an empty space in his brain, just beyond his thoughts, that he was trying desperately to reach. He shook his head to clear it.

"That presents a problem," he admitted.

"What presents a problem?"

"Taking me home. I'm not at all sure where that is."

The girl was visibly taken aback.

"You're not a vagrant, are you? I mean, you looked like you might be in pretty good shape, even if they had rolled you."

"I don't think I'm a vagrant, but the rolling, as you say, seems to have whammed some key items out of my mind; like where I live, or who I am, or, as a matter of fact, anything more specific than the capital of Australia, which I remember is Canberra, and some ideas about the current administration, which I dislike."

"Amnesia," she said, obviously thrilled.

"I guess so," George said. "It appears that we'll either have to turn me over to the police, which you all seem to want to avoid, or else I'll just have to sit here for a while and work at it." He looked at her, standing near the recorder, watching him with highly communicative sympathy. "I almost feel as if I can remember, if I only try hard enough," he added. "It all seems to be there, somehow."

"My name is Lynn—Lynn Harmony." It was a flat offer of friendship.

"Mine is—I mean we think, your mother and I, that mine might . . . George." As he said it, he rolled it around toward the gap in his memory; again, as before, there was a little sense of familiarity.

"That sounds awfully tentative, but I guess it will have to do."

"I guess so," said George. "Now, where am I? I know that sounds very Alfred Hitchcock, but it's the best I can do."

"What did Mother tell you?"

"She said we're in a basement apartment near the Park."

Lynn laughed, a half-arpeggio this time. "Mother is always being mysterious. The basement part is pretty right, but we're in the Park."

George was not sure he had heard correctly. "*In* the Park? Central Park?"

"Sure," said Lynn. "It's our summer home. We come here when the fortune-telling season slows up."

The conversation was decidedly not helping him regain what little remained of his thoughts.

"Your fortune-telling season?"

"You're worse than Mother's tape recorder. Didn't she tell you anything?"

"Not really."

"OK, I'll fill you in." She walked over to the cot and sat down near the foot, sitting on her right leg this time and dangling her left toward the floor. "You see, were gypsies."

"From Alabama? I didn't think they had gypsies native to the Confederacy."

"Oh, we're not really gypsies. Mother says we're professional gypsies. We read and advise, actually. That's what the law says. We read and advise, but it's really old-fashioned fortune-telling."

George was becoming more and more fascinated with this strange girl and her story. First of all, she was undeniably very attractive. At this range, she fulfilled all the promises of his first partial view and more. She was slim, but by no means undernourished—everything was very pleasingly scaled to a comfortable height, which George estimated to be about five-four or -five in the old tennis sneakers she was wearing. And her age . . .

"How old are you?" he asked irrelevantly.

"Twenty-three. How about you?

George groped, but could still not grope quite far enough. "Nice try. How old do I look?"

"Oh, I'd say thirtyish."

"Thirtyish it is, then. Now I've got a first name and an approximate age. At this rate I'll be cured in no time. Doctor, do you think I'll be able to play the piano afterward?"

"I know," said Lynn. "You're a violinist."

"Very funny. I suppose that being a gypsy, you would think of that. OK, so now why don't you start at what passes for the beginning, go on until you come to me, and then we'll play it by ear from there."

Lynn pulled up her left foot, tucked it over the right thigh in a passable half-lotus, and began to fill George in.

"About five years ago, Mother and I came up from Alabama on a visit to New York, and guess what we found?"

"Yankees."

"I thought we weren't going to be funny. We found

the place crawling with fortune-tellers. You couldn't go more than a few blocks in any direction without passing a reader, an adviser, a palmist, or a good old gypsy fortune-teller. Well, this gave Mother an idea. You see, Clayville, where we come from, is also crawling with fortune-tellers, only they're so much better than the ones we tried up here that we figured a real, no-nonsense Alabama gypsy could really clean up in New York. So, we thought, why should we pass this valuable knowledge on to someone back home, when this looked like a great chance to make good on our own? After all, Mother was in the local Little Theatre and I had been in some high-school plays—if we couldn't do the thing up, who could?"

"What about your father?"

"Oh, he could never pass as a gypsy for a minute."

"I meant, didn't he object?"

"Oh, no. He was never around often enough to object. As a matter of fact, we hadn't seen him for almost three years at that point, and I think Mother was looking forward to making it permanent. Anyway, when I finished junior college we packed our things, a crystal ball and a few palmistry charts Mother had bought in a second-hand store, some notes we had made of Clayville fortune-telling routines . . ."

"Folkways. Oh, sorry. I couldn't help it," he added, as Lynn tossed him a sharp blow with her eyelashed.

"All right. So we came to New York and rented a store down on the Lower East Side. We took turns shilling."

George was entranced. "And how did you do?"

"Miserable. It was the summertime, and we learned that city gypsies have a slack season in the summertime—I guess everyone is enjoying themselves outdoors or in Atlantic City or something like that. Anyway, we were evicted."

She waited for a comment from George, but getting

nothing but a bemused stare she took for interested attention, she went on.

"As I say, we were evicted. It wasn't too bad, being the middle of summer, but we didn't have much money left, so we came to Central Park and camped outdoors. Well, that is, we worked our way up to Central Park. It's the only park in Manhattan you can really live in, I mean. Gramercy is the nicest and quietest, but you can't always count on finding a child playing alone who will let you in. And Stuyvesant is terrible. But I'm wandering.

"Anyway, we came to Central Park and it was wonderful. We got to know all the regulars, and they always showed us the best camping spots—"

"Wait a minute," interrupted George. "What do you mean, *regulars*."

"The people who live here all the time, of course. There are lots of them. And one day Mrs. Spitzler told us about the Place."

"Mrs. Spitzler?"

"Mrs. Spitzler had lived here ever so many years. It was always rumored that she was fantastically wealthy, but eccentric, and that she preferred the Park to her duplex on Sutton Place or her estate in Palm Springs."

"That's what they always say about recluses and bums, I suppose. So what happened to Mrs. Spitzler?"

"One day she decided she was tired of living in the Park, so she shut up her Sutton Place duplex and retired to her Palm Springs estate. She was a lovely woman," Lynn added icily.

"I give up. Now, what about this place she told you about?"

"Mrs. Spitzler used to live in this place. *This* place," she emphasized, nodding her head in the direction of the unseen corners. "All the regulars knew she was here, of course, but otherwise no one really knows about it. They all hoped she would give it to one of them, but Mrs. Spitzler took a liking to Mother, and here we are."

"Where?"

"Oh, dear, that's right. We're in a large room—an apartment, Mother likes to call it, because it sounds more genteel—about a quarter of a mile from Central Park West at about Eightieth Street. That's the Belvedere Tower."

"We're in the Tower? I though it was a weather station, or something."

"Oh, it is. You see, this room is cut out underneath the stairs leading up to the Tower. We think it must have once been part of the Tower, but it must have been bricked up many years ago. That wall," she said, motioning once again into the darkness, "is brick. The others are whitewashed rock. Anyway, Mrs. Spitzler used to say it was made this way during Prohibition."

"We're *under* the Tower?" Somehow the idea of spending what was turning into a pleasant morning underground in the Park seemed rather curious, at least, to George. "You mean to tell me that you and your mother have been living *under* Central Park for four years?"

"Oh, no," Lynn laughed. "No, silly. We only live here during the summer. After Labor Day, we rent a store for the winter and tell fortunes. We usually let a few of the regulars, like Freddy or El Greco, stay during the winter, but we only live here summers."

"And how does this arrangement work out?" asked George, choosing to ignore El Greco for the time being.

"Not too badly. It doesn't look as if we'll ever be rich, I guess, but we make enough to break even in the winter—even to live fairly comfortably—with just enough to tide us over the summers in the Park. I don't suppose it has much future, but it's a lot more fun than Clayville."

"It would be," said George. "Would you mind if I asked some questions now? Just answer 'Yes' or 'No' while I try to work this all out."

"No," said Lynn.

"No, what?"

"No, I wouldn't mind if you asked some questions."

"OK, I deserved that. So, first. Your mother was working up some new routines on the recorder when I woke up, right?"

"Yes, she finds that new material—"

"Just 'Yes' or 'No' for the moment, Lynn, please. I've been absorbing a lot for the past hour. Now, the police, of course, don't know you're living here, which is why you were reluctant to call them for me."

"Right. I—"

"And you have no money?"

"No. Just enough to rent a—"

"How do you manage to eat, for openers?"

"Well, Freddy—he and Mother found you, you know—Freddy is a real whiz at gardening. He spent two years on a prison farm upstate somewhere. He says he should have been out in six months, but his tomatoes were so good that they kept him until his lawyer started to complain. Anyway, he's a real nut on organic farming—you know, manure, compost, and no chemical?"

"I know," said George.

"Freddy is a darling. He's got about a half an acre total planted all over the Park, in flowerbeds, under hedges, and even in the Shakespeare Garden, although there he has to put signs like *Leeks (Allium porrum) Henry V* on the onions, and things like that."

" 'I do believe your majesty takes no scorn to wear the leek upon Saint Davy's Day,' " whispered George, and again he felt a little flutter at the base of his memory, as if it were a bird held by one leg to the earth. And then he smiled, as Lynn answered, " 'I wear it for a memorable honor, for I am a gypsy.' "

"OK, my Welsh from Alabama, I think I've had enough for one sitting. Why are you telling me all—"

Just at that moment the lights went out, leaving the room in utter darkness. Before George could think of anything to say, he felt Lynn's hand slip into his.

"It's daylight," she said. "Let's go for a walk."

George felt himself being led to his feet and pulled across the dark floor.

"I suppose I can stand one more," he sighed. "What has the lights going out got to do with daylight?"

"We're tied into the Park's street-light system. See?"

George saw.

2 *How Hamilton Elincar Lost His Lunch and Will Shakespeare Reappeared*

Mr. Hamilton Elincar was a large ruddy man who habitually descended on Central Park about noontime to eat his lunch by the side of The Lake in rapport with Nature. He appeared to come straight from some kind of gainful employment, for he generally wore a tweedy suit of an indeterminate hue and a dully striped tie. This costume had caused the unkind to remark that he posed for cartoonists as Colonel Blimp.

A casual glance might discern some fairly strenuous, nonconstructive hobby in his appearance: perhaps Sunday soccer on Staten Island or an occasional fling at polo in Purchase. Certainly nothing more uplifting than riding to the hounds at those rare and infrequent opportunities when the call of the wild reaches the suburbs of Atlanta or Newport. Certainly not limnology.

Mr. Hamilton Elincar's hobby, however, was a diurnal and prandial affair. Over the crumbs of his neatly packed sandwiches, he delighted in spending lunchtimes by the waterside in the highly skillful and enjoyable pursuit of jamming transistor radios.

As a hobby, Mr. Elincar found this offered an appetizing range of delights to choose from: excitement, suspense, skill, courage, satisfaction. Excitement, as the obtrusive bars of a shrill rock-'n'-roll number audibly signaled to him that his lunch was being intruded upon by electronics. Suspense, as he twiddled the dial on his radiolike transmitter, searching for the offending station. Skill, as he manipulated his condenser and oscillator to give maximum annoyance to the squeals and buzzes that shortly began issuing from the offending set. Courage, as the hapless victim began to look around wildly for any possible source of his new troubles and almost invariably passed up Mr. Elincar, sitting aloofly on his bench, disposing of an apple, with a radio by his side and a plug in his ear— obviously listening to a quiet moment of Vivaldi or Buxtehude. Satisfaction, as the whining radio is shut off in disgust, leaving Nature once more undisturbed until the next signal—perhaps a bit of the President's press conference—begins the sport anew.

On this particular day he arrived about a half-hour earlier than usual and took possession of his customary bench at a point where the walk narrowed to only a few feet, giving him an unobstructed view of the broad sweep of The Lake from its edge, just beyond the walk, to where the blue water disappeared beyond a jutting clump of trees on the involuted shoreline. He grimaced as he arranged himself, for the faint but sharp thread of a hair-oil commercial was drifting across the water from a bench about three hundred feet farther down the walk.

Mr. Elincar placed the brown paper bag containing his lunch on the bench, took out his special radio, and extended the antenna. Then he put the dummy listening plug into his ear and turned it on.

He followed the sound carefully now, like a bird dog watching a falling mallard, while his fingers gently inched the pointer across the dial. He worked at it carefully, until the faintest whisper of a squeal came back to him across the water. Then he backed off, smiling an inward smile of radiance, and once more approached the crucial point. This time he rode through it; the whining on the interloping transistor radio reached a sudden ear-splitting peak and, just as suddenly, disappeared. *Now he's hooked,* thought Mr. Elincar. He moved in warily for the kill; slowly he brought his dial back to the offending station and listened to a rising volume of noise coming back to him from across The

Lake. Out of the corner of his eye he could see a man rising and attempting to shake a small object in all different directions and positions. Mr. Elincar laughed softly; adjusting his set for the maximum interference, he left it positioned there and turned up the volume.

Unfortunately, while he had been engrossed in this familiar, delicate maneuver, he had been approached unseen, by a duck. This is, Mr. Elincar did not see the duck, but the duck very definitely saw Mr. Elincar. Gliding up to the water's edge, this duck had emerged from The Lake and begun to waddle across the walk toward the bench. At that point Mr. Elincar was still making his first jamming pass and was intent on manipulating his control as expertly as possible. The duck, sensing this preoccupation on his part, made for its prime objective—the brown paper bag containing Mr. Elincar's lunch.

For Mr. Elincar was actually possessed of two sources of radiation that day: his doctored radio set, which could upset the tuning circuits of other radios at a range of several hundred feet; and two sardine sandwiches and a pickle, which could upset the olfactory circuits of a duck at a range of several hundred inches. And the sad fact was that he was too intent on the first to pay any attention to the later, until it was much too late.

It was over quickly—almost too quickly to sort out exactly what had happened. The duck clamped its bill on the paper bag just as Mr. Elincar reached the optimum point in his procedure. When he suddenly saw what was happening to his lunch, he jumped to his feet and tried to make a grab at the duck, who was waddling back to the water as fast as possible. Having missed his first grasp, Mr. Elincar lunged forward, dropping his radio to the ground just as the duck plunged into The Lake and began to paddle outward.

Mr. Elincar was now off-balance on two counts: his lunge at the duck, and his attempt to rescue his radio.

He might have recovered from both successfully if the radio had not quickly taken up the slack on the wire by which it was still attached to Mr. Elincar's ear. Now, the painful tug of a wire attached to one's ear by a plug, even if it is a dummy, is not to be denied. Mr. Elincar followed the tug faithfully, throwing up a great deal of water and spray as he hit the surface of The Lake. The duck, whose name was Hortense, paddled on, the paper bag held triumphally aloft.

Hortense came strolling up to George and Lynn where they sat in the grass beside The Lake, bearing the lunch she had fearlessly stolen from Mr. Hamilton Elincar.

George was laughing unrestrainedly at something Lynn had just said, and she was sitting calmly in her half-lotus position, waiting for the outburst to subside.

"Mercedes? And Carmen? Oh, no. You mean you can get away with names like Carmen and Mercedes Gitana, and no one even *suspects?*"

"Not at all," Lynn was saying. "As a matter of fact, I think that Carmen fits me quite well. Mother makes a convincing Mercedes, besides."

"But what about the blond hair? Doesn't anyone think that's just a bit curious."

"Not really. Gypsies are spread around enough to make anything possible. Besides, Mother always tells people that she was never sure who my father was, or where, for that matter. It holds together."

At this point Hortense dropped her rather pungent bundle in Lynn's lap. Lynn peeked inside and patted Hortense on her head.

"Sardine sandwiches for brunch, George. It's a good thing that Hortense doesn't like bread. She can always be counted on for good hunting."

She reached into her ample handbag—more of a leather potato sack with drawstrings, George had thought—and withdrew a small, curious fish, silver with a double black streak down each side. Hortense waited patiently; when it came arching her way, she snapped it up and wolfed it down, shaking her head violently. Then she waddled back to the water.

"Hortense is a dear, but if she filches too many lunches on any one day, someone may complain. As it is, they think it's a lark."

George was still thinking about the silver-and-black fish. "Don't tell me you fish these waters, too?"

"Oh, no. I carry these fish purely for Hortense. It keeps us friends. It's so hard to appeal to a duck on any other basis."

George attacked the first sardine sandwich, while Lynn uncrossed her legs, leaned back against an old willow tree, and began nibbling on Hamilton Elincar's pickle. The sun filtered down through the lacy green net over their heads; only an expert nitpicker would have been able to distinguish them from any other happy and hungry couple that had just had a meal furnished to them by serendipity, or by Hortense, for that matter.

They had left the Place, as Lynn called the basement apartment in Belvedere Tower, about daybreak and had been wandering about in the Park for six hours or so, stopping now and then to strip a berry bush or to dig up one of Freddy's carrots for a morning snack. Lynn had bubbled on and on about the advantages of Central Park for summer living and had tried to fill George in on the saga of the Harmonys of Clayville, Alabama; her effort left him with only a vague and confusing jumble on names, dates, improbabilities, impossibilities, and curiosities. At nine o'clock they had come across Freddy himself, a short dark man with a leathery tan and a nervous smile. He was dressed as an employee of the Park Department—regulation olive-drab trousers, short-sleeved shirt, visored cap with a maple-leaf insignia. rake; he was busy scraping manure from the bridle path.

"Hi," Freddy said, straightening up and leaning on his rake.

"Hi," answered Lynn. "I've brought you a patient."

Freddy looked up at George suddenly, as if he had just noticed his presence. "Hi," said George weakly.

"How's the bump?" Freddy asked.

Lynn had unwound George's muslin turban as soon as they had left the Place; out in the open, his mortal wound revealed itself as a lump the size of a chestnut, sitting in the middle of a crusty, matted, and extremely sensitive small area. George gingerly prodded the back of his head with his fingertips.

"Feels lots better," he said to Freddy. "I want to thank you and Mrs. Harmony for pulling me in the other night."

"Don't mention it," said Freddy. "I don't know what the Park's coming to, when a body can't even stroll around at night. It's cheap hoodlums like the ones that mugged you who give us all a bad name."

"Us all?" asked George.

"Freddy used to be a cat burglar, right, Freddy?" Lynn smiled at the short man, who nodded once and rested his chin on top of his rake.

"Upper-story man, as a matter of fact," he said wistfully. "You might not think it to look at me now, but I used to clear twenty, thirty thou a year—even after taxes," he added.

George was suitably impressed. "What did you—er—burgle?"

"Diamonds, mostly," answered Freddy. "Small, undistinguished diamonds, and lots of them. Always easy to get rid of. Also rubies, emeralds—anything that went on a necklace or a pair of cuff links."

"Pearls?" asked George.

"Never," Freddy said emphatically. "Couldn't tell the real ones from all the cultured and fake ones around."

"Tell George why you quit, finally," prodded Lynn. Freddy smiled his nervous smile—a tremulous upward twitching of the corners of his mouth, revealing a glimpse of several yellowish teeth.

"Well, I had just slipped out of a nineteenth-floor window at the Astor and I was inching my way along the ledge to the stairwell, so I could walk down, when I had a revelation."

"On the nineteenth floor?"

"I know it's a hell of place for a revelation, but I had one anyway," said Freddy. "I was hanging on with my fingertips between two bricks and my toes on the ledge and feeling pretty disgusted. It was a bad haul—two Tiffany brooches and a boxful of *schlock* tieclips, cuff links, and stickpins. Couple of grand was about all I could expect. Anyway, I was hanging on there in the airshaft, with the wind whipping around the corner of the building, and I said to myself, looking down, 'Freddy,' I said, 'this is one hell of a way for a forty-one-year-old man to be earning a living.' That was almost ten years ago, and I've been straight ever since."

"I love the way he tells it," Lynn said, "even though it may not be strictly the truth." Freddy looked pained.

"So the prison-farm episode came before?" George asked.

Freddy's look of pain deepened. "Ah, no. That was vagrancy. They got me my first year in the Park—before I learned the ropes." He gripped the rake and began drawing patterns with it in the cinders.

"And now you work for the city?"

"Not at all," Freddy said with surprise.

"But the uniform—" George began.

"Oh, that." Freddy smiled a wan smile. "Filched. It was my last job."

"Where's Mother?" Lynn asked suddenly.

"At the bandstand. She'll be back for dinner—we'll see you both then?" It was not so much a question as an invitation.

"Right," said Lynn.

"And as for that bruise, young man," said Freddy, "I wouldn't worry about it at all. Sun and cold water will do wonders—you'll be rid of that headache by noon."

"So long, Freddy," called Lynn, as Freddy resumed his quest for fertilizer. "He's Mother's boyfriend," she added to George when they were out of earshot. "I think he's cute."

"He certainly knows what it's all about," said George.

"You get around, you learn," said Lynn.

As the sun rose higher over the city, they watched the children come and go, the lunchtime office workers trickling in, the zoo guards feeding their guests, the squirrels, the pigeons, the bums, the elderly taking possession of their benches for the lonely day, and the not-so-elderly taking possession of their benches for, hopefully, a not-so-lonely day. Finally they had ended in the little grove by the water, hidden from the public by a thick row of willows and poplars and a high wire fence which cut the point off from the rest of the shore. They had entered it through a little building where gardening supplies were kept and which Lynn knew was never locked.

Carmen Gitana, alias Lynn Harmony, George was musing as he finished his sandwich. He wondered what he had been doing at this time two days before. He felt a now-familiar nagging memory fluttering around his brain, but the more he tried to grab hold, to look at it directly, the more it coyly avoided his touch—always, always staying just out of range of his thoughts.

"Nuts," he said aloud, jumping to his feet. "I'd like a hot dog."

"We'll go over to the bandstand and get some change from Mother," said Lynn, carefully burying the paper bag with the remains of Mr. Elincar's afternoon repast.

"Don't be silly—" began George, until he put his hand into his pocket and felt—nothing. Another feeling, a stranger presentiment of helplessness, clutched at George for a moment, but he shook it off. "Those fish. Are they for sale?"

"Of course," Lynn said. "So's the bag, and this sweatshirt, and—"

"Don't go too far," said George. "The fish are quite enough. Allez-oop!"

He hauled her to her feet and they cautiously made their way out through the gardening supply hut. George set a course for the zoo.

"Where to?" Lynn was saying, but George had his mind firmly fixed on a frankfurter; he found it strangely quieting to have something definite on which to concentrate. He tried concentrating on the mustard and the bun, too; it was just as good.

The seal pool is a round body of water surrounded almost entirely by concrete, a fence, and a few hundred gawking passersby for whom the seals are continually willing to replay their limited vaudeville act of diving, surfacing, and barking. George looked to see if there were any vaguely official-looking personnel about; then he pulled Lynn up beside him on the concrete abutment and began to talk in a voice pitched only a little louder than the ambient crowd noises. It was effective enough. Before he had finished his first sentence, he had about fifteen attentive listeners; that was all he wanted at the moment.

"Ladies and gentlemen. Every day crowds gather to watch our friends the seals being fed. You cannot really have been to the zoo without seeing the seals fed. Now, for only ten cents, you can feed them yourselves. Ten cents for a seal tidbit. Watch them run—er—float, dive, jump, and catch each fish as it's tossed to them. Ten cents a fish. You, sir. For the little boy?"

He plunged his hand into Lynn's handbag and came up with one of the tropical fish he had seen there. *Might as well use one for a shill*, he thought, and he threw it high out over the pool. As it hit the water the seals made a simultaneous leap at it and then gathered, barking, at George's end of the pool for more goodies. George's listeners, vastly impressed by this display, immediately produced coins in their hands and began pushing forward.

"One for you, sir. Here you are. Yes, ma'am. No, I'm sorry. I don't have change. Ten cents apiece, three for a quarter," he added with inspiration, "three for a quarter. Please don't push. Feed the seals, ladies and gentlemen. Here you are, sonny. That's twenty cents. No, I don't wrap them, ma'am. Just throw them right in the pool. Here you are, sir."

When the handbag emptied, George abruptly shut up shop and pushed away through a crowd that was building into disaster proportions. From the pool came the delighted barking of the seals as the between-meals treat came showering down on them like manna. And from the other side of the large knot of people, George could see two keepers bearing down curiously on the disturbance.

He and Lynn doubled back around the pool, skirted the cafeteria, and sat down in back of the monkey house to inspect the take.

"One dollar and twenty cents," he said. "Enough for two root beers besides."

Lynn was looking at him happily. "Poor Hortense," she said in mock anguish. "You've just sold her next week's food supply for a frankfurter."

Later, back in the shadow of the Tower, they sat on the high rock cliffs which overlook the small pond and the open-air Shakespeare theater. Garbled strains of Elizabethan music mixed with shouted stage instructions and hammering drifted up to them, and off to the right, the even fainter sounds of a baseball game, being played out in a broad vista of grass and trees, filled the warm air. George settled himself into a comfortable niche in the rocks and looked at Lynn, her blond hair framed partly by the bright greens of the Park and partly by the bright blues of the Manhattan sky, above the irregular shapes of the Central Park West apartment houses. She was watching the rehearsals far below with rapt attention, as if she were trying to make out every word of dialogue or instruction as well as every note of music. Her eyes were half-closed, either against the sun or to visualize better some long-ago world that was being reproduced below.

George could not help but reflect that he was happy.

How happy, he couldn't really say; he had no real standards of comparison before Tuesday night, and he certainly felt a lot happier now than then. But he also felt an undefined sense of happiness, as if, even if he could recall who he was and what he had been doing for the past week, month, or thirty years, he would still be happy at this moment, and probably very happy, at that.

There are moments that can be approached without any prior experience—moments which can be judged fairly, regardless of the background of heredity, environment, or newspaper editorials that have related them to the greater crostic pattern. Generally, billions of brief moments every day are categorized, pigeonholed, and tabled by a vast sensory network consisting of mothers' warnings, book reviews, a bad dinner once eaten, a train missed, a good investment, a poor investment, friends, and a broken shoelace or two. But occasionally one of these moments will bring with it all the information, experience, and knowledge necessary to appreciate it. Such a moment will flicker briefly in our consciousnesses with a rare glow, until a rush of opinions, half-remembered half-facts, and old photographs, like high scudding clouds snuffing out a brief flash of a warm winter sun, obscure the moment forever and relegate it to the "Miscellaneous" file in a ragbag of neurons and synapses.

George was curiously defenseless against these moments. His memory was well stocked with recollections—vague, amorphous thoughts and feelings of a lifetime—but he was lacking in beliefs, in feelings, in experience. And so a moment—this moment—shone for him in a cloudless sky; a happy moment which had neither beginning nor ending, but that simply was.

Vaguely, also, he wondered where he was supposed to be that day. An office, a factory, perhaps? No, an office, George decided. Somehow he felt as if he sat at a desk somewhere. He tried to picture himself sitting at a desk, and doing something—anything at all. Would he be writing? Dictating? Holding a conference? He thought about the papers he would be holding or the office in which he would be sitting, but they all leaped and danced just beyond his thought's gasp. *I should be someplace today, not here,* he thought. *But why?*

"Actually, you are a true gypsy, exchanged for a white-collar worker by a wicked troll while you were a child, and raised in The Bronx by well-meaning middle-class parents who worked to send you through N.Y.U.," said Lynn, unexpectedly breaking into his musings.

As he looked at her, startled, she added, "It wasn't very hard, really, to see what you were thinking about. Don't let it bother you, though. Any time you want, you can turn yourself over to the missing-persons bureau and get repatriated or whatever they call it. Or you can stay with us as long as you want. Freddy said these things are generally extremely temporary, and that one of these mornings you'll wake up with a personality."

"You mean I have no personality now?" George said with indignation.

"You know what I mean," said Lynn. "But I hope you'll decide to stay with us anyway. Look on it as a summer's vacation."

"But what about . . . where I work? They don't know I'm taking a vacation."

"Oh, they can't stay mad when it comes out you've had amnesia. It makes a convenient excuse when it isn't true—think how convincing it'll sound when it *is* true."

"You're right again. But tell me, Lynn. Why are you so anxious to have me around? After all, I may turn back into Dr. Jekyll at any moment, and ruin your little Central Park secrets. Suppose I'm a Secret Service man."

"Or a newspaperman," said Lynn. She seemed, for a moment, to be at a loss for words. "I don't know many people," she began, and then tossed her head in a little gesture of correction. "No, I don't mean that. There's Mother, and Freddy, and all the Park people, and the gypsies—they couldn't be nicer. But we wander around a lot, and I very seldom get to talk to anyone for any period of time. You know what I mean."

"I think so," said George.

"I've been able to talk to you today, and it's been fun. You've enjoyed yourself, too, and I don't think it would hurt anything, or hurt you, to hang around for a while. As long as you keep enjoying it, that is."

"I might be married," said George, injecting a not entirely irrelevant note into the proceedings.

"You're not wearing a ring," said Lynn logically.

"They might have taken that when they took my wallet last night," said George just as logically.

"You don't look married," said Lynn, resorting to female illogic. "Besides, Mother said I could keep you for a while."

"That's awfully nice of Mother." George was more gratified than amused by the turn the conversation was taking. "But I might have some ideas of my own."

"What?" asked Lynn partically.

George thought about it for a while and decided to change the subject. "Tell me, Lynn, are you used to keeping strange men who strike your fancy?" As he said it he was aware it sounded not quite right, so he tried again. "That is, do you generally stake out eligible male talkers for the season?"

"That's unfair," said Lynn, coloring slightly. "I'll tell you, maybe, when you have enough of your memory back to tell me what your pedigree is."

"Touché," murmured George. "OK, a bargain, then." A drum roll followed by a flourish of trumpets rolled up from the theater. He stood theatrically and raised his right hand. "I, George the First, declare this day to be the beginning of time, and that all happenings before this date shall be null and void, absolved, and kaput. From this time forward, until—er—circumstances dictate otherwise—" Aware that he was lapsing into officialese, he ended on a more up-to-date note: "—we pledge to play it by ear, and make up the rules as we go along."

"Chinese baseball," said Lynn.

"Chinese baseball," said George.

Lynn rose beside him, taking his hand in her own for a moment. "I don't think you'll regret it," she said softly.

George looked at her and then remarked, "You have mustard on your lip, you know."

Lynn laughed; standing on tiptoe, she kissed him briefly and tantalizingly. "So have you," she answered.

To George, it was a fitting part of his moment. He put his hands on her shoulders and began to return the kiss, but Lynn pushed him away and laughed again. " 'What, in the midst of the street?' " she asked.

The words were blocked out for George; he heard himself say them, accompanied by the now-familiar rustle of memory: " 'What, art thou ashamed of me?' "

Then they both turned on each other with the same thought.

"That's the second time—"

"This morning, the same—"

And, hand in hand, they began to walk down the hill, smiling over the familiar lines. "I seem to know Shakespeare, anyway," said George. "It may be a clue, but I don't know how good it is. It could just be a hobby, I guess." A feeling told him that it was a lot closer to the center of things than he could manage to express. An actor? "But you," he added, turning to Lynn, "how does an Alabama gypsy living in Central Park come in contact with old Will?"

Lynn nodded at the theater they were approaching. "Four shows a week, and free, for four summers. I told you I didn't have much to do." She looked at him strangely. "I thought I was getting pretty good, but you seem to be doing as well."

"Beginner's luck," said George. "Do you mean that you come to every performance?"

"Just about. It's right around the corner, and I can always pick up some trading stamps."

"Some what?"

Lynn looked puzzled for a moment. "Trading stamps. Mother and I collect trading stamps."

"That's nothing spectacular. So do millions of other people. But what has that got to do with Shakespeare?"

"We don't buy anything. We just pick up stamps. You'd be amazed at how many people dump stamps without even realizing they're worth real money. The Park is particularly good—people come in with goods they've bought and throw away the stamps, or women dump out the Kleenex in their handbags and out go some trading stamps with them. Men are worse, though. If you follow any man coming out of a store where they give stamps, three will get you five he'll dump them in the nearest basket. Mother, Freddy, and I are good for about one or two thousand stamps a week, not counting trades."

"Trades?" George was beginning to feel like the end man in a minstrel show.

"Well, there are several different kinds of stamps, and we can't collect them all. So we trade those we can't use with other collectors. There's a Prospect Park crew in Brooklyn that specializes in King Korn and S & H. This is just fine for us, since we tend to stick to Plaid and Royal Purple. They're all worth about the same, so we trade on a one-for-one basis. Freddy trades with them about once a month when he goes out there to get their pigeons."

Every time he brought up a new subject with Lynn, George had the distinct impression he was taking a swim in a lake composed of quicksand, molasses, and tangled seaweed: a verbal Sargasso Sea.

"I'm being shipwrecked again," he said. "Let's wander into the Globe, here, and see if we can straighten all this out."

They straightened it out in hushed whispers as the players, dressed in scraps of costume and street clothes, ran through isolated scenes interminably. The play was *A Midsummer Night's Dream,* and George felt it was particularly appropriate.

One of Freddy's many provisioning sidelines involved the distribution and sale of pigeons. A ready supply was available for poaching in the city parks, and Freddy had developed a regular route among some of the less reputable restaurants in the Columbus Circle and Broadway neighborhoods that were delighted to be able to feature squab on their fly-specked menus at reasonable prices. Actually, they had assumed that Freddy's birds were products of golden grain and hormones under the tender care of the Connecticut sun; Freddy did little or nothing to cause them to question that assumption. And not all of his clients were catering to the lower-middle eating classes—an expensive neighborhood hotel had been a steady customer until the chef found his lost cuff link in the gizzard of one of Freddy's birds. Nevertheless, Freddy maintained his local routes, furnished with birds abducted bodily from the Central Park shrubbery or imported from Brooklyn. "They're quite good, too," added Lynn. "Occasionally we eat some ourselves—on special occasions, of course."

"I see," said George, somewhat dizzied by all this activity. "And do you have any other income supplements besides pigeons, vegetables, and telling fortunes? I suppose that you sell, once in a while, your trading-stamp premiums?"

"No . . . that is, we generally find it easier to pawn them. It only realizes about a quarter of what they're worth, but it's awfully hard to go around trying to sell one pair of bookends."

"It must be frustrating when you have a few half-full books, and just not enough to redeem. I suppose you have bad weeks."

"Oh, we do." Lynn looked around, as if she were about to whisper a schoolgirl secret. George was looking at her curiously and was half listening to the words coming from the stage: "My lord, I shall reply amazedly, half sleep, half waking: but as yet, I swear, I cannot truly say how I came here . . ." Her voice came to him as he was thinking that he, too, had been transported to a bewitched world in a dream; that the part he was acting, for this moment, had been written just for him.

"When we have a bad season, or need extra stuff, we generally print the stamps ourselves."

3

How George and Lynn Talked with Puppets and El Greco Spoke of Art

"You print them yourselves?"

There seemed to be very little George had been able to add to the conversation except for a persistent echo of Lynn's last lines. Psychiatrists and poll-takers may be paid for that sort of thing, but George was just becoming confused.

"Not on a big scale, or anything," said Lynn, hastily. "A few here and there, just to fill up a few books more or less. I'm sure it really doesn't hurt anyone; it sometimes gets pretty difficult to turn up the last few stamps of the right kind."

Somehow, everything this girl and her mother had been saying was very definitely English, but George was finding it difficult to make any kind of twentieth-century sense out of it all.

"What the hell are you talking about?" he asked.

"Well, some years ago Mother got the idea of forging trading stamps to help out with our collections," Lynn began patiently. "After all, they looked pretty simple, and no one ever examines a whole book full of them, anyway, So we asked El Greco to make copies for us."

"El Greco the painter?"

"Yes. He's a doll—he lives and works in an abandoned tennis-equipment shed just north of the reservoir. He said he would be glad to, so we fixed a price with him—I think it was about twenty-five cents a thousand stamps, or something like that—and when Greco needs pin money he'll run off fifty or so sheets for us. He thinks it's all very commercial and beneath him, but he does it because he likes us."

"How does he do it?"

"Oh, I don't know. Some kind of etching or screening, I guess. But the copies are great, and he puts in the serial numbers by hand. Once, when it had been raining for a couple of weeks and he couldn't get to work—"

"Which is—?"

"Which is sketching sidewalk portraits in the Village—he ran off enough stamps for us to get a radio, and the redemption center never even blinked!"

"How come you don't do this on a large scale?"

"That would be illegal," said Lynn ingenuously. "Besides, Greco won't do it regularly. He doesn't need the money that often; he says it isn't professional. But we have a printing press, and one day, when we learn how to use it, we can get this business started on all cylinders."

"And where do you keep this printing press?"

"In the puppet house. Like to see it?"

George would like to see it.

The puppet house turned out to be an old frame building in the Park, not far from the Tower, Lynn produced a key from her jeans and unlocked the door. "They'll be gone until next week," she said. "They're on tour."

The house was dark and cluttered and smelled of cut wood—a marvelously pungent odor that made George think of model airplanes and sawdust. The puppets were ranged neatly about the walls in various states of construction: Punch, Snow White, Pinocchio, Judy, and a plentiful assortment of ogres and witches. At the far corner of the room in which they were standing, a plain wooden puppet stage with white muslin curtains was built against one wall. It was a slight disappointment to George, who always remembered puppet stages as being brightly decorated, but it fitted in with the works-in-progress atmosphere of the rest of the shop. Farther on, through a half-open door, he could make out racks of costumes of various sizes, from baby puppet to full-size human.

"This is my very favorite place in the world," Lynn was saying. "I feel that my life is as make-believe as theirs; sometimes I spend hours here playing with the puppets on that stage or just trying on the costumes and pretending."

"What do the owners think?"

"Oh, they're a puppet group run by the city. They don't know anything about me. I have a schedule; I only come in when they're out. Once I had to hide in the attic for three hours when they came back unexpectedly, but usually it works out fine. There's the printing press."

It was a small offset machine, standing in one corner next to a tidy pile of advertising circulars. It was obviously used to run off the troupe's publicity and seemed to be in a good state of repair. George walked over to it. As he did he could feel his scalp tingle with *déjà vu*; he knew he had once done this all before. He adjusted the paper feed, selected a metal plate from the table alongside the press, wiped it down, fastened the mat on the drum, and ran off a few tentative copies. He worked as mechanically as the offset press. The clack-thump-clack again stirred a light touch against his memory, as if it were trying to say *remember, remember, remember*. A printer? A printer? He thought over the clues he had. The name George. Printing. Shakespeare. He sighed. Nothing quite fitted.

The copies were good. He switched off the machine, cleaned the mat, and put the copies on the pile with the others. Then he looked around.

Lynn was gone.

He started for the other room but was stopped by a high-pitched voice from the stage.

"George, come here, you clever man. Come here, and let me kiss you."

He wheeled around and saw the puppet Judy leaning perilously over the edge of the stage, beckoning to him with a small, mittened hand. "Come, George. Come, George, you nice man."

"Judy! Judy! Who are you talking to, Judy?" Punch leaped to her side, carrying his long slapstick and shouting in a voice reminiscent of a cleft palate filtered through a kazoo. "Stay away from other men, Judy. Judy belongs to Punch!"

"But he's so beautiful. I want him!"

"Watch out, Judy!" *Wham!* The slapstick laid Judy flat on the stage apron, but she bounded back with vigor, and snatching the slapstick away from Punch, began a pitched battle that raged all around the proscenium—a battle that produced, as sound effects, the *thwack* of the stick, the raspings of Punch, and the tantalizing warnings of Judy. George laughed and applauded until his palms hurt as Lynn came smiling from behind the stage, bowing slightly—her hands still encased in the two personalities who, just a moment ago, had been creating a furious world of mayhem in the tiny picture frame. George stood up, still applauding, and suddenly Lynn was in his arms, her lips pushing hard against his own, and then he was holding her tightly to him, kissing every available square inch of her eyes, nose, ears, and lips while she folded her arms around his neck and their breathing rose and fell together.

"Oh, George," she was whispering, "I think I'm falling in love with you."

"You are a nut," George nibbled into her ear. "A one-hundred-percent, dyed-in-the-wool nut, and you're wonderful." He pressed his mouth onto hers for a moment and was briefly startled by the spectacle of Punch peering over his left shoulder. He looked around and saw Judy staring over the right. He laughed, setting Lynn down carefully.

"How long have we known each other, Carmen?" he said.

"Oh . . . about ten hours, I should say."

"And you don't have the faintest idea who I am."

"You're George."

"Or Sam. Or Albert. Or Cuthbert."

She laughed her little-girl laugh up the scale. "You couldn't be a Cuthbert. You look like a George."

"Well, you shouldn't be so careless about going all out on such short notice with anyone who looks like a George. He may turn out to be an Oscar."

Lynn held up her left hand, and Punch made a little bow. "Mr. Punch thanks you for those kind words of advice to a poor young, misguided virgin," she said in the rasping puppet's voice, "and awards you the Flower of Womanhood Seal of Approval. Anyway," she continued in her own tones, "I just wanted you to know where you stand. If you hang around, you'll have to get used to fighting me off."

"I'd be delighted," George said quickly, meaning that he'd be extremely delighted.

She kissed him once more, lingeringly, on the edge of his lips; as George moved in closer, Judy hit him a *whack* over his head with the slapstick. "That," said Lynn, "was for calling me a nut."

She began to put the puppets back in their places on the wall rack. "By the way, how did you do with the printing press?"

"Fine. We're in business."

"You mean you can work it?"

"Every knob and dial. I must have been born to it."

"What luck. You turned out to be a printer."

"Or a forger. Which would be more appropriate. The next problem is to make the plates."

"In that case," said Lynn, "we're off to see Greco."

"We're off," echoed George. How far off, he was not sure, and most certainly did not even suspect.

"The trouble with Art today is the museums. It is as simple as that," said El Greco. "The museum is a prison, no? It takes the poor little fragile colors and *clang!* it locks them up in dark stone dungeons. The color cannot live like that, yes? It must be free. Free to breathe in the sunlight. Free to soothe the eyes and the hearts of all humanity. Not jailed like a drunk in the tank for twenty, fifty, a *hundred* and fifty years of solitary confinement. *Pah!* A mausoleum it is, not a museum. The Metropolitan Mausoleum of Art. 'Freedom!' cries the government. And then it locks up all those poor paintings in their jails. Sunlight is what they need. Sunlight and love. Not neon and guards."

George looked thoughtful. "You know, I never—"

"Shut up," said El Greco. "I'm talking about Art. Capital 'A'. Always capital 'A'."

El Greco, whose real name was Stavros Kyriekides, was a small dark man of about sixty years; he wore a pair of slightly bagged brown trousers and a corduroy sports jacket, belted in the back, that must have dated from the Armory Show. A few wispy strands of gray hair were smoothed back over a bald spot, which was surrounded by an erratic black fringe. Even his face looked rumpled; the massed wrinkles ran from forehead to jowls with the inevitability of the Nile flowing to Khartoum. Still, behind a pair of rimless lenses, held together by some silver struts and a piece of picture wire, shone the eyes of a man with a Mission.

"What would happen if every car made in Detroit was bought by a rich collector and put in a museum, hey? All those automobiles in museums, behind a rope. Don't touch! Don't smoke! Don't look too long, you'll wear out the chrome, yes? No, this would be criminal. Give the people their automobiles, but lock their Art up in prisons."

"But there are car museums—" began George.

"Decadence, decadence," muttered El Greco. "We live in decadent times. Automobiles in museums. Vacuum cleaners in museums. Beautiful Art in museums. Pretty soon we all will live in museums, in glass cases, like prisoners. Sentenced to life imprisonment in a museum. What did *View of Toledo* ever do to deserve that? I ask you, now? *Mona Lisa?* A rapist, even, gets time off for good behavior, or can get a parole, but the *Angelus?* Never. What do you want?"

"El Greco, this is George—" Lynn started.

"I'm in a hurry, child. Tell what you want of Greco, and then Greco can get back to his poor prisoners."

It would all begin with the frame. "In a six-inch plaster-and-gilt Empire frame," El Greco had once said, "I can pass off a dollar bill as a Gilbert Stuart portrait." He had started his crusade as a penal missionary by making a careful survey of the Metropolitan collection, during which he noted, as groups, all paintings of similar size cased in similar frames. Then, for each group, he would construct an all-purpose frame—one that might easily pass for any of the four or five in that particular lot. Greco's frames, however, had one important peculiarity: the seemingly massive rococo structures folded into packages that could be carried conveniently, if a little awkwardly, in a trouser leg. Then he was able to begin his campaign in earnest.

First, he photographed his quarry in the Met. A fast thirty-five-millimeter shot generally sufficed, because "who will notice anyway, yes?" Then, in the cellar of his shed, he began to work with the color slide. After making an enlarged color print the size of the original painting, Greco projected his slide onto a piece of canvas; using the projector as a *camera lucida,* he began slowly to block in the details. From photo to finished painting, sometimes as long as six months elapsed. "I must age it, no? My audience may be fools, but I have my professional pride."

El Greco had worked out the next series of events very carefully and could bring them off with the precision of the Navy backfield. A typical evening schedule on D Day looked something like this:

4:30 P.M. El Greco enters museum with both the substitute painting and the enlargement wrapped around his body, and the frame in his trousers.

5:00 P.M. Museum closes.

9:15 P.M. El Greco emerges from men's room. He has spent the last few hours in a stall, assembling the frame and straightening out the photograph.

10:00 P.M. As soon as the nearest guard has finished his rounds in the gallery where Greco is going to work, the artist steals up to his quarry, removes it from the wall, and replaces it with the color photograph in the folding frame. ("So who's to know? The guard, he's an art critic, hey?")

10:45 P.M. Greco retires to the nearest unused utility closet, where he embarks on the most difficult part of his assignment, while the cleaners go through the building mopping and scrubbing ("But not looking at paintings, yes?").

The crucial work which occupies El Greco from 10:-45 P.M. to as late as 3:00 A.M., depending on the difficulties he encounters, must remain a trade secret. However, the problem—removing the Metropolitan's painting from its stretcher and frame and then substituting the original El Greco—is solved with skill, dedication, and love. Also, as he had once hinted, with staples.

Circa 3:00 A.M. The real frame is returned to the wall with the substitute painting. The folding frame, the photo, and the real painting disappear into the men's room with El Greco.

3:15 A.M. The painting and the photo are wrapped around his body; the folding frame, folded, goes back in his trousers.

10:30 A.M. *Exeunt omnes.*

In the bright sunlight that streamed in through the windows of a small attic in the abandoned shed where he worked, Greco pored over the fruits of his eleven-year compaign: three Rembrandts, a Vermeer, two Cézannes, a Lautrec, two Goyas, three Millets, two Holbeins, four Corots, and a Monet. Almost two paintings a year had been liberated from the prison and brought to freedom in his shed. For this was El Greco's life, his work, his secret, and his crusade.

"Why should they suspect?" El Greco would say indignantly. "Who would dare come to these prisons really to love a painting—to feel its life bloom for them? That takes years and warmth. The guards see the

painting, but they look through it. They would not rec-
ognize a subway poster if they saw it. And the
people. *Pah!* What do they know about gesso and
grounds, glaze and beeswax? Nothing, yes? Less than
nothing! They stare and they glare and they read their
guidebooks. It is the right shape and size and color, no?
It has a nameplate? Then it is it."

"But, Greco," Lynn had once asked him when he
was in a rare and expansive mood, "why such a strange
collection? If you like Rembrandts, there are more. The
same with Goya. Why such a grab bag? Why don't you
specialize?"

"Specialize, specialize! You would prefer I be an
eye, ear, and throat man? Don't bother me with this De-
lacroix, I am a Rubens man, yes? But as long as you
ask, my child, I will tell you. It is all in the frames."

For that, of course, was the secret of El Greco's
choices. He had found that his folding substitute frames
were generally more difficult to make than the paintings. And so he used them again and again, until all
works of Art which appealed to him, and whose frames
happened to resemble his own, were safely in his attic
cupola.

In eleven years he had used five frames for nineteen
paintings—"It is a credit," he said, "to the uniformity
of what passes for thought in a museum that a Van
Gogh can be framed almost identically with a Rubens."

And, except for the amount of time spent crouching
in the Metropolitan's bathrooms, El Greco considered
his business evenings rewarding and constructive. Rewarding, because another imprisoned painting had been
freed. Constructive, because he still had his frame and
could start planning on the next conquest—of the same
size.

This was the artist to whom George was suggesting
the forgery of trading stamps.

"Those cursed stamps again, and here I am in the
middle of a Whistler. I have told you, dear child, that

when I feel so inclined, I'll make some pieces of pretty
paper for you and your lovely mother. But it's up to El
Greco. Now, go!"

With a broad sweep of his arm, he knocked over a
can of murky turpentine and began absentmindedly to
massage the colors into the floor with his left toe.

"There's money in it," said George.

"How much?" said El Greco, his manner changing.

"I'll have to clear it with the Voice—I mean Sally—
of course, but supose we say, tentatively, ten percent."

"Tentatively I'm a seagull and I'm flying, hey? Ten
percent of nothing much is nothing doing. Out."

"Oh, Greco, sweet," Lynn said, turning on the charm
until George was nearly blinded and even Greco took a
step backward. "Oh, Greco, sweet, we're not asking for
much. This may be our big chance. George really
knows how to handle the press over in the playhouse.
We may be able to turn these things out by the thousands. Who knows? And you wouldn't have to do any
work other than make the plates in the beginning."

"And put in the serial numbers," added George.
"That shouldn't take long."

"Serial numbers, yet? When will you learn that nobody looks at anything. A Rembrandt, a trading
stamp—it's all the same. Soon the trading stamps go
into the museum, yes? The colors are right, everything
in the right place—the stamps are hokay. We can print
the serial numbers on."

"They can't all be the same!" protested George.

"Who looks?" Greco shrugged his shoulders. "Maybe
a few numbers, then, as you say. We make five different
numbers so you can mix them up a little, hey?"

"That might work," George reflected. "That would
be seven plates—one for each color and five for the
numbers."

"I make you ten plates, even—Greco gives three
more numbers for free."

"Then you'll do it?" Lynn asked.

"I didn't say I wouldn't," said Greco.

"Greco, you're a doll," said Lynn exuberantly. "If George weren't here, I'd kiss you."

"Oho, so that's the way the wind blows. Well, my child, in that case, if the young man weren't here, I'd kiss you. Meanwhile, everybody down to the cellar for business."

Greco led the way, and with Lynn holding George's hand, they filed down a ladder at one corner of the room into the basement.

Greco's darkroom was grotto about twenty feet square, half taken up with moldering tennis nets and court rollers. At one end he had set up his photographic equipment, which consisted of an old studio camera with a long patched bellows and a modern-looking slide projector.

"I got that for about ten thousand of my own stamps. I should go into business for myself instead of working for you slavedrivers."

He fumbled around in one corner of his equipment, among a collection of old bottles, half-filled trays, and piles of scattered papers. Finally he found the transparency he was looking for and set the projector and camera facing the whitewashed section of wall he used as a screen. As the light was switched on, George and Lynn saw a sheet of Royal Purple trading stamps magnified in front of them.

"We use Royal Purple because it is easiest," said Greco. "No fooling around wtih curlicues and portraits. I make a sheet of two hundred stamps or so, and you can run off as many as you want."

"We're in business," said George.

"Not so fast," said Greco. "You have to advance me the money for the plates. I can't make an offset master on scrap metal, hey?"

George looked at Lynn. "We'll ask Mother," she said. "Or sell some more fish for the seals."

"Here," Greco was saying to George, "here are the plates I've been using to keep these thieves in guitars for the last few years. Here. It's no Goya, but it's quite good enough, no?"

Yes, George thought, *it is quite good enough.* The two-color plates had been meticulously etched; they were already worn with repeated pressings. The copies, he surmised, had been made on an old hand press that stood in another corner.

"This time it'll be a lot easier for you," George promised. "Just ten plates—all photography and no etching—are all we need."

"Decadence," sighed Greco. "No more is craftsmanship respected."

"You'll have just that much more time to liberate the Whistler," said Lynn.

"Ayy, the Whistler. It is so beautiful. I hear they have another like it in storage. If I could only get into storage, I could even leave the photographs. Nobody ever looks at those poor solitary prisoners down there. If I could only get down to their storage, I could free a painting a month. A painting a week!"

Even in the gloom of the cellar darkroom, lit mainly by the sheet of Royal Purple trading stamps projected on the wall, they could see Greco's eyes flash with hope and longing. The Metropolitan's storage rooms were his one dream, destined to be as unfulfilled as are so many of our one dreams.

"We had better go," said Lynn.

"Yes. You will give me cash for some offset plates and I will make you such beautiful stamps you will give me more than ten percent of nothing, no? And I will give you two maybe a Rembrandt for your wedding."

"We've only known each other for twelve hours," said George.

"Twelve hours, twelve years, twelve dollars. What does it matter? If you love each other, you will be warm, like the Rembrandt. You will have light, like the Rembrandt. You will be priceless, like the Rembrandt. Twelve hours can be a lifetime. The Rembrandt was in prison for more than twelve times twelve years, and you should see how sunlight and love has made it a living thing again. Twelve hours, *pfui*. Maybe I give you a Millet. It's not nearly so priceless."

"You're wonderful, Greco," said Lynn, "and I will kiss you."

She kissed him on the forehead and began to climb the ladder to the main room. "You see," said Greco to George, "when a pretty girl kisses you on the forehead, you know that she's married, has a lover, or you are getting old. I know that I am getting old."

They climbed back into the comparative brightness of the studio. Greco looked around the littered room for a moment and at the white canvas on the old easel—a white canvas blocked in faintly with lines, shapes, and tiny notations. "And that you do not know who you are matters not either," he said to George. "I—I have been wanting to know for years who I am, but I think I will never find out. My paintings are nothing—*trompe l'oeil* amusements for an indifferent audience of high-school students and museum guards. *Pah!* Greco is no artist. My copies are not even good copies, but they serve their purpose. They allow the true genius of Degas, of Cézanne, to breathe fresh air once again. For them I am satisfied. I only paint for them. Next to the real El Greco, I am but a poster painter. Next to Van Meergeren, I am but a journeyman copier. Next to myself—"

He trailed off and stared softly at Lynn for a moment before turning suddenly away with an impatient gesture.

"Out, thieves. Bring the money and El Greco will make you stamps. But first comes Whistler."

As they left, laughing and hand in hand, they could picture him one night, perhaps five or six months in the future, spending three-quarters of the dark time from dusk to dawn crouching in a stall of a Metropolitan Museum of Art washroom.

"OK, darling, now let's roll the presses."

4 *How They All Went Fishing*

Cool, tall, and elegant, Sally Harmony presided over her table with a grace that was singularly inappropriate to both her company and her surroundings. She took the role of hostess seriously and had dressed for dinner in a simple one-piece tan jumper, from which the collar of a man's white shirt peered unobtrusively. The atmosphere was festive, but every once in a while George felt Sally gazing at him as if he were a crystal ball; he twitched nervously as he mentally checked all his buttons and zippers. He found Sally's habit of making occasional remarks in her sepulchral soothsayer tones quite disconcerting; several times he fought an impulse to answer, "Isn't it so, sister," or, "Amen," when he heard her eerie request to please pass the butter. Once he succeeded in knocking twice on the underside of the table with his foot, but he found, with a strange thrill, either that nobody noticed or that nobody cared.

The table was set in a corner of the Place. Two formal candles accounted for all of the light, partly for atmosphere and partly to conserve the automobile batteries that supplied their power when the street lights were off. The dinner was excellent, consisting of vegetables from Freddy's gardens, a fish appetizer (on whose origins George could only speculate), and a medium-rare steak. This last, George discovered, came not from a herd of cattle hidden in the Park but from a local butcher. It was anticlimactic and delicious.

The company consisted of George, Sally, Freddy, and Lynn. Freddy had changed from his purloined Park Department uniform into slacks and a rather colorful sport shirt. George and Lynn had decided to see a Shakespeare performance later that night—George was wearing an old jacket that Freddy had lent him, together with a tie and some other accessories which had belonged to the mysterious Mr. Harmony and which Sally had been keeping, out of sentiment. The conversation tended to be disjointed. George kept sinking into his favorite preoccupation—his identity—while Lynn, for some mysterious reason of her own, added to his confusion by blithely talking about him in the third person. More than once George noticed he was thinking of himself as *George*, instead of *me*. Contributions from each of the four wandered aimlessly back and forth, generally emphasizing individual matters of utmost interest to each of the participants.

". . . manure. But if I forget to mulch the raspberries again tomorrow, my dear, I might just as well forget the whole crop this summer . . ."

". . . the butter. Please pass the . . ."

—*Isn't it so, sister*. ". . . clues present themselves, but somehow I can't grasp their meaning. Like Shakespeare. Printing. Things like that. I'm sure I can break through if I . . ."

". . . plastic-wrapped monstrosities they call fruit, all full of DDT and sprayed with wax to look shiny. What's so terrible about a worm now and then . . ."

". . . getting on to the end of August already. We must think about renting a store for the winter. I think Lexington Avenue in the Eighties or Nineties might be . . ."

". . . scrape all the Vitamin B away and then try to put it back with all sorts of strange chemicals and . . ."

". . . Labor Day at the latest. All my customers will be back from Atlantic City. However, I'm behind on my scripts. Maybe Madison Avenue in the . . ."

". . . the lights went on . . ."

". . . let's have our coffee and talk about George's project . . ."

Sally had frugally blown out the candles, and now she began to clear the table, while George explained the plans he had been working on since he and Lynn had visited El Greco that afternoon.

"It's quite simple, really," he said. "Lynn tells me we can count on at least five days next week at the puppet house. We'll have to work during the day—at night someone might notice the sound of the press. Allowing enough time to straighten things out every day, cleaning the press, and the triple run for colors and serial numbers—that should let us print about five thousand sheets."

"Two hundred stamps to a sheet, Mother. Can you imagine. A million stamps! We're rich."

"It's not that easy, Lynn," Sally said. "But let's see what it would be worth. A million stamps, right, George?"

"Right."

"So, that means about five hundred to seven hundred books. What stamps are you using?"

"Royal Purple," said Lynn.

"Good old Royal Purple," threw in Freddy. "I hope this doesn't make the Prospect Park crew mad—they're a good source of pigeons."

"Let's consider the advantages first, dear," said Sally crisply, and Freddy dried up in a flash. "George, if you can run off your five thousand sheets, I daresay we can turn over about five hundred dollars on them. That's assuming about two thousand in merchandise at the redemption center and about a three-quarter loss turning them into cash—that includes selling the pawn tickets," she added practically.

"Better on cameras?" asked George.

"A little," said Freddy, "but not much."

"Well," said George, "that's it. Greco said he'd have the plates as soon as we give him some money in advance, and then we can give it a whirl."

"Wait a minute, boys and girls," Sally said thoughtfully. "George can certainly run off his five thousand stamps in one week, but that doesn't mean we can cash them in all at once. I don't even think we can paste that many into books."

"That's reasonable," George agreed. "Besides, you could never get that many stamps past the redemption center without a lot of curiosity."

"How many the first week, George?" asked Sally.

"I would say about a thousand sheets should do it. You would clear about a hundred bucks, and I can store the extra stamps here until you get around to pasting them up. A hundred, a hundred and fifty books would be plenty the first time out, I guess."

"It sounds too good to be true," said Sally. "If we can clear a hundred a week—"

"Minimum," said George.

"That remains to be seen. Nevertheless, if we can clear a hundred a week for the rest of this summer and all of next—"

"Why can't we keep it up during the winter, Mother? After all, trading stamps aren't necessarily seasonal."

"First of all, we don't need the money during the winter. We do fine in the store. Second, there's not that much profit if we have to think about finding another printing machine or another source of paper and ink for the asking. The puppet house is closed during the winter, and we couldn't take a chance on using it."

"I guess you're right," Lynn said reluctantly.

"What about perforating?" asked Sally.

"I was coming to that," said George. "Greco has a block with some nails driven through it that he's been using for his runs. It's a little awkward, but if we all work together we can manage. We have to mix up the serial numbers, so that means plenty of tearing and pasting, anyway."

Sally was making some calculations in a notebook. "Yes, that's a hundred and fifty books, at least. That means we're going to have to scout around and pick up enough blanks in the next few days, without looking suspicious. Starting tomorrow, then, we cover the Royal

Purple stores. There are about thirty in midtown, so
let's say five books a store would be right. I'll cover the
East Side from the Plaza. Freddy, you better hit the
West Side. And Lynn, you can work your way down to
Times Square until you get—oh, say about fifty or sixty
books."

George felt as if he were initiating a wartime advance. "I'll check the press out again tomorrow and
work with Greco on the plates. If he starts in right
away, we can be ready to roll tomorrow afternoon."

"I told you, I have to mulch the raspberries tomorrow, Sally," complained Freddy, but as the crystal-
gazing beam was turned his way, he added hastily,
"OK, OK—but I'll have to start late. Besides, I got a
pigeon route to make tomorrow," he mumbled.

"I think cameras and wristwatches would be best for
this effort," Sally was saying. "Musical instruments are
too unreliable. Goodness, that reminds me, it's almost
seven-thirty." She consulted her watch (four and one-half
books) and began to remove the coffee cups from the
table. "You two had better get on line if you want to get
seats. By the way, what are they doing this week?"

"*Midsummer Night's Dream*," said Lynn.

"*Midsummer*," sighed Sally. "I played Helena for
five performances in Clayville. 'Ay, do, persever, coun-
terfeit sad looks; make mouths upon me when I turn my
back; wink each at other; hold the sweet jest up; this
sport, well carried, shall be chronicled.' "

Freddy opened his mouth to speak; for one dazzling
impossible moment George thought he was also going to
begin a recitation. But instead he said, "Sally and I
thought tonight would be a good night to go fishing. Do
you want to come along?"

"That's right," said Sally. "All I have in the freezer is
about half a dozen small ones for Hortense—I'm all
out."

"Which of the lakes do you fish in?" asked George.

"Come along and you'll find out," Sally said.

George shrugged his shoulders. "Why not? When will we meet you?"

"About midnight. Central Park West and the Transverse. It'll be a dark night," Freddy added.

"Enjoy yourselves, my dears," said Sally as Lynn checked the coast through the peephole and then, taking George by the hand, slid outside and closed the old door. The queue began just down the hill; there were about a hundred people already waiting for the gates to open. They varied in type from elderly gentlemen, sitting on collapsible seats while their wives packed the remains of picnic dinners into neat beach bags, to scraggy schoolgirls in turtleneck sweaters, tights, and micro-skirts who had come from The Bronx to pass as Greenwich Village hippies; from dating teen-agers, dressed impeccably for the theater but hardly for Central Park, to a host of inconspicuous men and women whom Lynn knew and pointed out to George as local residents.

"That group comes from the north part of the Park—I think they live in a cave near the Loch, or someplace. I don't really know them too well. Mrs. Frisbey, there, lives in the bandshell, in a room next to Freddy's. Freddy says she snores something awful and drinks herself into a stupor every day. Oh, hello there, Mrs. Frisbey! How nice to see you! Old bag. Oh, and there's Maria. Maria really lives in Rockefeller Center, but she spends weekends in the Park, and she's almost a member of the family. That bunch of people there comes up from Washington Square. They live in the Arch—it's hollow, you know. Lord knows what they all do in there."

This flood of incredibilities would have staggered George a short time before, but now he merely experienced a little dizziness, as if his sense of belief was teetering on the edge of a sheer cliff, from which the long plunge into absurdity was just a footstep of crumbling earth away. He noticed, however, that these friends and acquaintances of Lynn's were, on the whole, distinguished by their indistinguishability—they were dressed reasonably and could have come from reasonable apartments or houses rather than from, it seemed, every nook and cranny of Manhattan Island.

"Living in a public place is not the easiest thing in the world—it's vaguely illegal, for one thing, although I don't know if anyone has ever tested the public's right to live in public parks. But anyway, if a person were conspicuous enough to be noticed, it wouldn't be long before someone began to suspect that he was spending an unusual amount of time hanging around. So, the gray-flannel squatter emerges."

It figured, George thought. Protective coloration operated as well for humans as for birds or lizards. As long as they blended into their background, they became unnoticeable. For a moment he felt the heavy lost feeling that had first come to him when he realized that his identity had been stolen with his wallet—a numbing hollowness that crawled out of his stomach and opened painful emptinesses all over his body.

But in a moment it had passed with Lynn's glissando of laughter, as they stood patiently while several hundred additional theatergoers queued up rapidly behind them.

"Oh, George, I am enjoying myself so. Will you stay with us even when you—when you find out about yourself?"

How could he answer that question? And yet something in him wanted desperately to say "Yes." "I would have to be in a hell of a good situation before even considering not staying," he said ambiguously.

A look of momentary pain flashed through Lynn's eyes, and he immediately felt sorry for not just having said what he knew he wanted to say. "Please don't ever consider it," she said. "What could there be that is so much better than this?"

And, with a toss of her head, she included it all in *this*: the Park, the night, Shakespeare, Hortense, feeding the seals, Freddy and his pigeons, Mrs. Spitzler, the Place, El Greco, the lady in the bandshell, the summer sky, Manhattan, and, most of all, herself.

"Nothing," George heard himself say. "There can be nothing else."

There was a low rumbling noise inside the circular walls of the theater; it grew louder and louder, until, suddenly, the gates opened and a rush of people poured over the surrounding paths like a flow of lava from an erupting volcano. They hurried in a great swarm like lemmings toward Central Park West, as if to remove themselves as quickly as possible from this dark and strange world of earth, grass, and rustling trees into the comfort and roaring life of the stage-lit city. Nervous at every unknown shape, terrified at every unknown sound, they scurried toward civilization—eager to dodge across the avenues between shrieking automobiles, to dive into the rumbling, screeching world of the subway.

George and Lynn climbed the path up toward the shadow of the Tower, gaunt against the starry sky. The forest thoughts of the play continued with him into the forest life of the Park, as he turned Lynn's question and his answer over and over in his mind. What *could* be better than this? If he knew, could he—dare he—make a choice? "How did you like it?" asked Lynn.

The answer seemed to come to George very easily. "An altogether admirable production, except I really don't know why Oberon's makeup had to look as if it had been applied with fingerpaints. And the comic touches are more reminiscent of Uncle Miltie than Sweet Will. But all in all, it was quite enjoyable."

As he said his pat piece, he felt the crawling finger of *déjà vu* touch the fringes of his thoughts again. *Somehow this is important too*, he thought.

At the words, Lynn had turned to look at him sharply—a touch of puzzlement appeared in her glance, as if she had bitten into a strange fruit and received a very familiar taste, but one she could not exactly place. George was unaware of the effect his remarks had had on Lynn. He was trying to pin down the floating uncertainties that were still slithering around just beyond his reach.

"I didn't quite understand your point," said Lynn strangely.

"I'm not sure I did, either," said George with a forced laugh. "It seemed to mean something more when I said it."

They entered the Place by the little boarded-up door, which swung open at the turn of Lynn's key, and in the moment before switching on the lights he held her to himself. They stood against the stone wall beside the closed door—her head tightly against his chest, his lips brushing the part in her hair. He knew that her whole body was clinging to him. It was a feeling to rank with the most acute of pleasures—the feeling that another person, another personality, another human being is holding on to you. Then he turned on the lights and Lynn stepped back.

"I'll change in your room," she said, her eyes glittering. "We don't have enough time for monkey business."

His "room" was an alcove about seven feet square in one end of the long chamber. It had been used for storage, but Sally had put a screen across its opening and had put the cot inside for George. Sally and Lynn slept in the main room on a double bed pushed against the wall farthest from the door and covered, during the day, with a black drop cloth and three brightly colored pillows.

He lay back on this bed now, his head against one of the pillows, while Lynn gathered up a pile of clothing and disappeared behind the screen.

"Don't get any ideas," she called. "Just because Mother isn't here to chaperon us doesn't mean I can't defend myself."

"I defend my right to have any ideas I want, at

least," said George. "The fact that they all involve you to a more or less erotic degree has nothing to do with the matter—this is a free country."

"That's not nice. You're supposed to put me on a pedestal."

"I can think of more comfortable places."

"The trouble is that you're decadent. I've decided that you work in advertising, or something like that. You have no initiative. Madison Avenue men are all alike—they haven't the guts to begin something, but once they're dragged into it they keep it going for years without ever thinking about getting out. If you had any moral fiber, you'd storm over here, rip down the screen, and make passionate love to me."

"Where did you learn so much about Madison Avenue?" asked George, sitting up. "Besides, you shouldn't talk like that. I'm only two days old, and you could be charged with impairing the morals of a minor."

"It's too late, my love. If your morals weren't impaired just a little in your previous life, you probably wouldn't be half so interesting. Besides, again, I'm all ready."

She stepped out from behind the screen wearing a tan print blouse with an out-of-focus pattern and a pair of well-tailored brown slacks. The blouse was open at the throat, displaying a loosely knotted kerchief.

"My fishing costume," she said. "I'm sure Izaak Walton would approve."

George was struck once more by her gracefulness as she walked across the room toward the door.

"Coming?"

He touched her in a moment and they kissed heavily—George searching in her lips for his own identity, for himself.

After a while Lynn darkened the room and opened the door.

"We've got an appointment to keep, and it's late," she said almost apologetically.

George smiled. "I've got some angles of my own, my darling, and they don't all involve baiting hooks."

"Want to bet?"

All appeared to be quiet on the grounds of the Museum of Natural History. A soft wind rustled the leaves of the surrounding trees and lost itself in the darkness below. A trained observer, preferably equipped with a sniperscope, might have been able to distinguish the shadowy shapes of four figures flitting from tree trunk to tree trunk in the dim half-light of the stars and the Manhattan skyglare of neon and tungsten.

All four of the interlopers wore trousers, but (and here is where the sniperscope would have come in handy) two of them were apparently women. One of these seemed to be the leader—an imposing middle-aged woman who was incongruously dressed in dungarees and a black leotard. She was squatting under a tall oak at the northwest corner of the museum's wall, watching a smallish man juggling an extension ladder against the tree. The two figures completing the quartet were younger—they stood holding hands behind a thick hedge against the museum's rear wall and seemed to be fairly oblivious of the enterprise going on not more than a hundred feet from where they stood. They were dressed with considerably more taste than the other two; nevertheless, they were involved in some way with the effort, for the smallish man was trying to attract their attention while he maneuvered the ladder around the base of the tree.

If it was help he was looking for, it did not come in time. As he was signaling to the young man with one hand and trying to straighten the ladder with the other, he caught his foot in a root and went down. The ladder fell with him; the four figures disappeared abruptly into the underbrush as the ladder's crash echoed through the deserted grounds.

After some ten minutes of electric silence they reappeared. This time the two men were together, the smaller whispering furiously to the younger. They retrieved the ladder and set it up against the oak. The older woman resumed her squatting position, and the girl stood lounging against the marble walls, one hand in the pocket of her slacks, the dark blur of her face outlined by a soft frame of golden hair.

"Women and children first," hissed the smallish man, who had a narrow taxi-driver's face surmounted by what could have easily been a taxi-driver's cap. The girl went up the ladder first and stepped off the top rung onto a broad branch that bridged the distance from the tree to a second-floor set-back roof on the museum. She crawled swiftly on all fours along the branch until she was over the edge of the roof, and then dropped lightly down.

The woman went next, scrambling up the ladder and over the branch with easy, practiced movements, dropping beside the girl. An argument seemed to be taking place on the ground now, which ended with the young man climbing slowly and carefully up the ladder. As he shakily transferred from the last rung to the branch, he froze. The woman waved to him and the older man shook his fist, but he remained standing uncertainly at one end of the branch, hugging the trunk with obvious love and affection. Finally the man on the ground joined him in the tree, and after a brief discussion the young man ventured out on his hands and knees.

He progressed with irregular, dreamlike movements, somewhere between those of a deep-sea diver and a tightrope walker. Halfway across, he stopped again—he had made the mistake of looking straight down at the dimly lit grass and shrubbery some twenty-five feet below. It would have been better if he had frozen. Unfortunately, the next thing the watchers saw was the young man dangling over the side of the main branch, clutching a smaller branch with both hands and swinging his feet helplessly in the air.

The women suppressed a brief cry; the older woman and man crawled out from opposite sides of the branch until they met at the point where the younger man dangled. There was a brief whispered conversation, in which the young man played a heated part; they grabbed both of his wrists and sat facing each other. The hapless climber hung between them.

Finally they all proceeded to take part in a strange form of locomotion. The seated woman would inch herself backward on the branch as the older man inched himself forward; the dangling man, like the hook of an overhead conveyor, was slowly and surely carried to the museum roof, where the girl was waiting to clutch at his legs.

After a few minutes of silence, broken only by the scrape of trousers along the bark, she clutched, the couple on the branch released, and all three dropped down to the roof.

"Are you all right, George?" the girl asked the young man anxiously.

"I'll live," George replied in a whisper, "but I don't know how the hell I'm going to get back."

"Don't worry," the man in the cap said. "Sally and I carried you here, and if we have to, we'll carry you back."

"Right," Sally. "Let's go."

The four figures—Sally and Freddy leading, with Lynn and George bringing up the rear—proceeded to make their way up two iron ladders set into the walls, until they had reached the top floor of the museum. A large skylight was set into the roof; it looked down into a room in which only a small night light was burning.

George peered through the panes of glass and could dimly see many glass tanks, large and small, arranged in rows across the room. The tanks were filled with fish of all shapes and colors; the glass panels carried various plates and tags.

"The tanks on the other side of the room are for experiments," Lynn said. "We checked that with a small telescope once. Red and yellow tags mean that some sort of scientific hanky-panky is going on; we give those a wide berth. The tanks on this side of the room seem to have healthy specimens only—a few now and then are never missed."

Freddy found the pane of glass for which he had been looking. Using the blade of a penknife, he gently pried up the wooden molding, revealing a strip of masking tape holding the glass in place. He removed the tape and the glass, setting them carefully on the roof next to the molding. At the same time, Sally opened a small metal box she had been carrying and took out a long line with several fishhooks tied to one end. From a plastic bag in the box she chose a few slices of fish which had been taken from their remaining stock. She baited the hooks and turned the line over to Freddy.

Spreading full-length on the edge of the skylight, Freddy lowered the line into a likely-looking tank directly underneath the open pane. George, looking on nearby, saw a sudden churning in the water and heard the agitated sound of a distant piscine fight. Freddy cursed and pulled the line up as fast as he could. They all gathered around to inspect the results.

The bait was gone, and so were two of the hooks.

"Piranhas," muttered Freddy. "Wouldn't you know."

"We've still got some bait left—we can try again," said Lynn.

Freddy was unconvinced. "It means we'll either have to open another pane or use the rod."

"Let's use the rod," said Sally. "If it doesn't work, then we can worry about another opening."

Freddy reached into the box and brought out a small fishing rod in three sections. He fitted two of them together, strung the line along its length, and then, dropping the whole apparatus through the open pane, extended it over the next tank and lowered the hooks. This time there was no immediate reaction. George could see, dimly against the water, the shadows of several fish warily circling their unexpected midnight snack.

In a short while there was a tug on the line. Freddy jerked the fish out of the water, swung him over the piranha tank, and hauled him up. "You've got to bring 'em up over a tank, or there'll be too much water on the floor," he explained to George.

The fish came up flopping. It was one of the silver-and-black-striped ones that George had seen at the Place. "More food for Hortense," Lynn said happily.

"I guess we'll feed her first," said Freddy.

Sally stunned the fish with a blow from her shoe and dropped him into a large laundry bag which had been stuffed into the metal box. "Number One," she announced.

Numbers Two through Twelve were handled in the same easy manner. When Freddy noticed that the population of the tank had been depleted by about half, he switched over to another. This time he brought up, with considerably more effort, a large, rather ugly spotted fish with what seemed to be long flowing mustachios.

"Attaboy," he said encouragingly. "We've hit the cat-fish tank."

Sally looked pleased. "They're used for scavenging," she said to George, "but if we can get them before they're put in other tanks, we know they've been raised on good, wholesome fishfood. The museum raises the best catfish for eating in the world."

Freddy quickly brought up six or seven catfish, and then Sally took over the line. She was good for two more before they decided to switch tanks again.

"Doesn't anyone ever notice missing fish?" asked George.

"If they do," said Sally, "they either suspect each other or they're too afraid to call attention to the possi-bilty of marine cannibalism. Anyway, I don't think there have been any major repercussions. Thar she blows!"

This last was directed at a good-sized red-and-brown fish with prominent red and blue dots and a mean expression. Freddy whistled.

"Brook trout! We're really in business."

A dozen or so denizens of the brook-trout tank

quickly fell under the heel of Sally's shoe; the laundry bag began to take on the exploded-population look of a fish-store window. Finally Sally sat back with a sigh and began massaging her right arm.

"I think, children, that we've finished. They should last us until we shut up shop for the summer."

"One more, Mother. I want to try that tank just to the left, there."

The tank Lynn was referring to was in the deepest of the shadows, but they could all make out several shapes moving to and from in the turgid waters. "One more it is," agreed Sally, and she turned the line over to Lynn.

Lynn took her place on the ledge and dropped her hand through the opening. With the rod extended over the tank, she lowered the line into the middle of the circling shapes. There was an immediate reaction.

One of the shapes caught at the bait and gave a tug that pulled Lynn's arm in through the opening up to her shoulder. George immediately began to haul her back. Meanwhile, Lynn clutched at the rod, tugging at what was only visible now as a thrashing blur.

"Don't drop the rod," hissed Freddy, "or they'll know what's up."

Lynn didn't. She fought like a professional, holding the rod inside the skylight, while George added his weight to her pull. Freddy reached through the opening and grasped the line.

There was an ear-splitting crash as the tank toppled, spilling water and three mako sharks across the laboratory floor. The one Lynn had hooked measured about two feet in length; George saw that they could never have gotten it up even if they had wanted to.

"Hold the rod," Freddy repeated grimly; he began sawing on the line with his penknife; the shark was twisting at the end, swinging back and forth like a pendulum. As Freddy slashed through the line, Lynn and George toppled over backward, and the shark, as amazed as any of them, dropped with a towering splash into the piranha tank.

The piranhas, not quite pleased by this intrusion, attacked; as the four anglers gathered up their gear and fled down the ladder, they could hear the distant din of the mako holding his own. Freddy stayed just long enough to put the glass and the molding back into place, and then he, too, scrambled out of sight.

His disappearance was none too soon. A light inside flashed on, revealing to two puzzled guards the strange sight of the wreckage-strewn laboratory and a Herculean struggle being waged by a shark inside a tank which had contained only piranhas at quitting time.

Sally, Freddy, Lynn, and George scrambled back across the branch, down to the earth, and out of the museum grounds as fast as they could.

"I hope the line disappears in the fight," Freddy said as he replaced the ladder in the little equipment shed from which he had borrowed it.

Lynn, flushed and excited, was still holding one section of the rod in her hand. "Congratulations," said George. "You almost landed a real one."

Lynn knew the answer to that. "I'm after bigger game," she said.

Lynn sat on her bed with a scrapbook in her lap, her head whirling with indecisive thoughts. It was a large, old-fashioned book into which Lynn had been pasting her memories of New York: advertisements for movies she had enjoyed, matchbook covers, theater programs and newspaper reviews, menus.

She and George had come back to the Place alone, laughing and in good spirits. Sally and Freddy had gone off to Freddy's room in the bandshell; Lynn knew enough of her mother's habits to be sure she was gone for the night. Normally this would have delighted her, especially in the present circumstances. But tonight she wanted to be alone with her scrapbook for a while, for a very special reason.

They had returned and put the fish away in the freezer. They had talked. They had talked about each other, about the Park, about each other, about fishing, about each other. George had been persuasive and Lynn had been swaying, but in the back of her mind something else was bothering her. And now George was lying, presumably asleep and frustrated, in his little alcove, while Lynn curled up with her scrapbook and her thoughts.

Since the early part of the evening, a strangely familiar sensation had been nagging her; with the finality of jugsaw pieces falling together correctly, she finally knew what she had been recalling. Before her, on top of the closed book, lay the newspaper clipping at which she had been staring. She had saved it, as she had saved every other item about the Park's Shakespeare productions for four years. Particularly, her attention was riveted to a sentence which ran:

Although the players have, as usual, put together an altogether admirable production, it is hard to see why they have chosen to skimp on so many physical aspects of the mise-en scène. Oberon's makeup, for instance, looked as if it had been applied with finger paints.

And to another:

The mood was quite enjoyable throughout, even if the comic touches appeared to be more reminiscent of Uncle Miltie than Sweet Will.

The floating phrases which had bothered her all night sat firmly anchored to that crumpled piece of newsprint. In the whirling questions that now assailed her thoughts, one fact stood out with clarity—a fact that seemed to have a single meaning at times, a fact that was difficult to interpret in many different ways.

Across the top of the cutting a line read *NEW YORK ALARUM*, and this particular article was headed *"OFF-BROADWAY*, by George Revere."

Revere. Revere. Revere. Revere.

The name echoed and reechoed through Lynn Harmony's mind. Was this the name? Or had he read the same review? Could the George be a coincidence? But wouldn't this explain the printing? The Shakespeare?

Would it? Could it? *Revere. Revere.* Was it? *Revere.*

She stuffed her hands into her ears, as if to stop the flood of unanswerable questions. Slowly she got off the bed, tucking the scrapbook and the clipping under her pillow. She walked over to the screen in front of his alcove.

George Revere. She ducked inside and stood staring down at his sleeping form. He lay on his back, one arm flung around his head, the other stretched across the covers. His breathing rose and fell regularly; he breathed heavily, as if the weight of his unknown identity were pressing on his chest. *George Revere.* She raised her glance to his key ring, which hung from a nail driven into the whitewashed wall. Sally had put it there the night before, in hopes it would remind him of something—of anything. She took the keys in her hand and brought them outside, feeling them, one by one, as if to extract some secret. Then she put them under the pillow with the clipping and turned off the light. She stood for a long moment in the darkness, listening to the rhythmic breathing. *George Revere.*

She slipped inside the alcove once more. A decision had been made. Without taking her eyes from his face, she drew the top of her pajamas over her head and let it drop silently to the floor. Then, shaking her hair loose, she stepped out of the trousers. *George Revere.*

Gradually she lowered herself to the edge of the bed, still without taking her gaze from his face. She leaned over him and kissed him softly—softly at first, then harder as she heard him stir and felt his eyelashes open against her own. His arm moved to her back and he quickly drew her down and down.

Oh, George Revere, she thought. *Oh, George.*

How Sol Berman Praised His Marketing Department and Lynn Took a Bath

Central Park lies along the middle of Manhattan like an elongated pool table, its green felt torn, twisted, and scarred by a never-ending succession of weekend amateurs. The Lake is the third of these major scars, reading from top to bottom. It is roughly located in the northern half of the area that would be enclosed by a bank shot from the Metropolitan Museum of Art off the Museum of Natural History and into the Plaza fountain. Although such a cosmic carom might have startled a visitor to The Lake very early one steamy August morning, it would hardly have fascinated him as much as the sight of a naked young man with a duck on his stomach floating in a cove about five feet off the opposite shore, one hand shading his eyes from the first slanting rays of the sun appearing above a Fifth Avenue cooperative.

The young man was obviously enjoying himself. He was in an excellent mood, and he paddled back and forth in the greenish water, tingling in the slight night chill remaining in The Lake. Suddenly he twisted and dove, throwing the duck off his stomach with a fluttering splash, and then abruptly surfaced, raising his angrily quacking companion on his head. The duck, nonplussed, slid upside down into the water, one twitching foot enmeshed in the man's hair. Over they both went, the duck fluttering and quacking, the man chuckling.

He swam slowly around the little cove, while the duck watched from the branch of a sunken log, momentarily out of the clutches of this maniacal sea creature.

The young man relaxed in the cool green buoyancy. He stroked quickly to the far shore, in a reasonably passable crawl, and then floated back again, his hands cupped behind his head, his eyes closed. The duck quacked once more, impatiently, and the young man reached into the tall grass that grew to the water's edge, bringing out a small silver-striped fish in each hand. The duck leaped off the log and skimmed quickly to the man; the silver fish described bright arcs against the overhanging trees before disappearing into the flat orange bill. The young man rolled over on his back and resumed his slow paddling from one side of the cove to the other, with the duck once again peacefully riding on his stomach, until the early-morning sun began glinting off the water. Then he hauled himself up onto the soft moss and earth of the shaded clearing.

"I love you, Hortense," George said kindly to the rear end of the retreating duck, and began to towel himself vigorously, rubbing out the early-morning chill of The Lake with the rough friction of cloth on skin.

He dressed quickly. When he had finished, he peered cautiously across the little arm of The Lake. There was no one in sight. He slipped under the fence which guarded the peninsula from the public, pushed the wire links back into place, and began a half-mile stroll that took him past The Mall and down into the maze of paths, tunnels, and bridges that make up the crazy quilt that is the southeastern section of the Park. The sun rose still higher, until it hung, impaled, on the grotesque minaret of the Sherry-Netherland. George felt an impulse, fortunately controllable, to make his way to that unbelievably futile tower for the purpose of greeting the rising sun and the rising citizens of the city with an appropriate call of "Allah akbar" or, perhaps, "baksheesh," which was the only other Arabic word he could think of. Instead he stretched out on the wide railing of one of the pedestrian bridges across The Pond, threw a crumbling piece of cement into the still water, and conscientiously devoted the next few minutes to watching the ripples regenerating themselves from the center, where the pebble had disappeared, as they traveled slowly to either shore.

It would be churlish not to come right out and say that George was happy. It would not only be unfair to him, but it would invite a horsewhipping by being unfair to the girl who was directly responsible for a mood that made all things, even the roof of the Sherry-Netherland, possible.

"Lynn," he said at one point earlier that morning, "I love you."

"Uuuuhhhh," Lynn had said.

"Delightful," said George, and he had kissed her eyelids and then the left side of her nose. "Lynn, I am going to leave you here alone to welcome your Mother home, because I know she'll see in a minute that I've done her little gypsy wrong. From my inner radiance, I mean."

"Uuuuuunnnhnhnhnh," said Lynn.

"So I am going for a swim in The Lake, and then I will throw myself into the printing business at hand. You will join me later at the puppet house."

"Aaaarrrrruuhhhnn," said Lynn with feeling.

"Until then, my sweet. I love you."

"Rrrrrrrrrrr."

And now, as the sun climbed higher and higher, George ambled aimlessly under the trees, through the hedges, and over the grass. If he had had the least expectation of getting a coherent answer, he would have said *hello* to a gray squirrel sitting on the statue of Balto, the hero of Nome, and munching on a cigarette package. If he had known, he would have blown a kiss of gratitude to Andrew Haswell Green (1820-1903) American lawyer, b. Worcester, Mass., who had been instrumental in rescuing one hundred and fifty-three square blocks from the grubby fists of the tenement builders and dedicating them to the worship of Gaea.

"Attaboy, Andy," he would have said. "I know just how you felt."

He looked around, in passing, at the morning crowds filling the park—screaming children with bored mothers, tired old people soaking up the sun like blotters, middle-aged men and women whose worn shoes or worn looks stamped them as members of the jobless.

"Who the hell are they?" George thought. "Do they really know who they are, any more than I know who I am? As a matter of fact," the idea struck him, "I bet I'm a hell of a lot more *me* at this minute than anybody here.

"I can lick any identity in the house," he murmured with a grin, earning a startled look from a woman who was shepherding two small cowboys past him.

"What's in a name?" Lynn thought as she closed the door of the telephone booth behind her and took the directory down from the rack. Outside the glass cubicle the Central Park West traffic moved uptown in regular waves, to the cadence count of the traffic signals. Inside, there was an unnatural quietness, as if the noise of the morning world was filtering through several layers of blankets. It was also blisteringly hot—the August sun beamed happily through the booth's glass walls and rapidly turned it into a personal steam cabinet.

Lynn leafed quickly through the pages until she came to the "R"s. There were five possibilities, but relying on her feminine instinct and a shrewd hunch, Lynn chose the two who lived nearest to the Park. A. G. Revere lived on East Seventy-fifth Street, off Fifth Avenue, and a George Revere was listed at West Eighty-seventh Street near Columbus. She took a deep breath and dialed G. Revere.

A woman answered and her heart dropped.

"Hello?" came that most unhelpful of all questions.

"Mr. George Revere, please," said Lynn.

There was a momentary silence. "Hey, you musta got the wrong number. The only Mr. Revere here is Giuseppe, and he's not home."

"I'm sorry," said Lynn quietly, and hung up. She had

one more possibility, if her hunch played out correctly, and she dialed again. A few blocks from where she was standing, a phone began to ring to an empty room. Standing in the booth, Lynn listened to it ring in her ear five . . . six . . . seven times, and then replaced the receiver.

"Either he's single or his wife works," she murmured, sliding the door open and walking determinedly up the avenue.

She found the house for which she was looking about halfway down the block. It stood first in a row of identical brownstones, pushing the belly of its bay window out over the sidewalk. Scars around a large parlor-floor window showed faintly where the front entrance had once stood at the top of a flight of vanished stone steps. In the downstairs hall a rusty mailbox carried the white-on-black legend: *George Revere—2A.*

She stood for a moment in the hall and thought of her slow return to consciousness that morning—the throbbing stretch that drained the last ounce of sleep out of her body. She remembered her sudden alarm at finding him gone, followed by a soft feeling of tenderness as she recalled, as a dream, his kisses and his voice promising to meet her. She thought of the bursting happiness of washing, the sweetness of dressing, the warm joy of the sun as she waited for her mother outside the Place.

"How's George?" Sally had asked, and Lynn had answered, "He's gone to see Greco about the plates." And that had been that.

Now she stood outside a door that might be his; she fingered, for the fifth time, the key ring lying in her purse.

"Looking for someone?"

Lynn felt as if she had been propelled a good six inches toward the ceiling by the question; she took a deep breath and was amazed to find herself standing securely in the same spot.

"Mr. Revere," she said.

Her interrogator was a rumpled man in his sixties, wearing a two-day stubble of grayish beard and a battered suede jacket. He was holding a key in his hand. Lynn could read SUPERINTENDENT emblazoned all over his person in letters of oil and burned-out light bulbs.

"Revere?" He appeared to consider the possibility for a while. "The young fella ain't been home for a couple of days—he ain't in now."

"Oh, that's all right," Lynn said. "I have an—an appointment. I've got the key."

The old man's eyes twinkled for a minute, then he closed one abruptly. Lynn saw, to her horror, that it was supposed to be a broad wink.

"Oho," he said, "so that's how it is." He pointed at 2A. Lynn took out a key at random. It didn't work. She made an effort not to look around, out of fear that he would wink at her again. The next key fitted. She pushed the door open and quickly closed it behind her, catching the fleeting beginning of the old man's chuckle as he returned down the stairs.

That awful old man, Lynn thought, but her brief annoyance gradually gave way to delight at being in George's apartment: the age-old feminine pleasure of knowing something that someone else did not know. This momentary feeling in turn quickly changed to curiosity. George's three old-fashioned rooms occupied the front half of the parlor floor; the ceilings were high, the fireplace was deep, and the bloated bay window afforded a brief glimpse of the Park at the end of the long block. Lynn spent the next half-hour examining, with unflagging fascination, everything from the laundry bin in the bathroom (one sheet and two white shirts with incredibly dirty collars) to the fireplace in the living room (an old hammer handle, two cracked boards bristling with rusty nails, and the ends of a Seven-Up box). In the bedroom she inspected a portable typewriter that stood next to the tangle of the unmade bed, and peered with interest at the sheet of paper in the machine, and at its cryptic message:

DETROIT, DETROIT!
by
George Revere

Shaking her head, she picked up from the floor a heavy piece of T-shaped metal formed to spell out the name **GEORGE REVERE** and brought it back to the living room, where, in the rickety eight-leg desk, she found an appointment calendar (*Wednesday—Ginny*!!, *Saturday—Valerie***!, *Tuesday—Sylvia***?).

With this last artifact in her hand, Lynn stretched out on a comfortable sofa. The problem of decoding George's arcane system of asterisks and exclamation points fascinated her, expecially as she realized, not without a twinge of painted jealousy, that *Sylvia***? might have been involved with George's mishap in the Park.

Had she steered George into its shadowy depths so that an accomplice could rob him? Or had George been taking her home? (Through the Park? So late at night?) Was she his type? What was his type? Who were *Ginny*!! and *Valerie***! Would she be *Lynn*! or *Lynn**, or *Lynn*? Was she hungry?

Yes, she realized with a start, she was hungry. Rising from the sofa, she pitched the offending calendar into a corner of the room and headed for the kitchen, leaving her shoes behind. She felt a comfortable sense of being at home, padding around his apartment. The first faint realization of a noble feminine emotion that illuminates and complements the tenderness of love was beginning to stir in her soul: namely, possessiveness.

"Once I get this plate fixed," said El Greco, "everything will be perfect."

George watched quietly while the artist carefully wiped the metal mat with his fixing solution and held up, for their inspection, a glittering surface on which the images of one hundred and ninety-six Royal Purple trading stamps (in fourteen rows of fourteen) were placed.

"A Rubens," murmured Greco. "A Monet."

George could not help agreeing. The two plates Greco had just finished represented the backbone of their cooperative publishing effort. He had finished the yellow background mat earlier; now, with the purple finished, he had just the serial numbers to complete before the first run could be made.

"How long?" asked George.

"How long?" snorted Greco. "How long did it take Leonardo to capture the ineffable smile of La Joconde?"

"Joconde?" George asked.

"I use the French," said Greco. "How long did the great Michelangelo work over each fold in David's slingshot?"

"How long?" echoed George, playing the game.

"Twelve years," said Greco. "Twelve years on a rotten slingshot, my son, and you have the nerve to hurry an artist over a mere offset plate. I should destroy it immediately before it makes materialistic Philistines of us all."

"Well, how long will it be before the first serial numbers are ready?" said George imperturbably.

"Forty-five minutes," said El Greco, "and then we can break for lunch."

"Forty-five minutes," said Sol Berman, president and general manager of the Royal Purple Trading Stamp Company, "and then we can break for lunch."

"Yes, Mr. Berman," said the director of his marketing staff, a Princeton boy who confided to his mother that he knew a great deal more than Mr. Berman; he did not tell her that this was mainly in the area of when to say "Yes" and when not to say "No."

"OK," said Berman, twirling the point of a No.-3

pencil around inside his ear. "I want you all should know you've done a good job. It ain't the best, mind you, but thank God it seems to be working fine."

It was very unusual, if not difficult, for Berman to do anything but hurl curses at the little group now standing huddled around his scarred wooden desk on the fifth floor of the Royal Purple Trading Stamp Building. Actually, Berman's Bazaar, as it was clandestinely known to the working staff, was not housed in as grandiose quarters as the name might suggest. Royal Purple, which had started in a telephone booth outside Macy's some four years before, occupied a decrepit Park Avenue South loft building that had previously housed a publisher of flagellation magazines. Curious items of erotica still came to light, now and then, in broom closets and dumbwaiters, giving the staff something to talk about on their long and frequent coffee breaks.

"I employ nothing but Pierpont Morgans and Follies girls," Berman would say repeatedly, pointing at a gathering around the coffee wagon. "See? That's not coffee they're pouring, it's my blood."

He reserved choicer phrases for his marketing staff, a group of college and advertising-agency trainees who had obviously never heard of Barney's or S. Klein. "A half a page with nothing on it," he would scream, waving a trade journal apoplectically. "You're killing me, you doctors, you." (Anyone who pretended to know more than Berman or dared to exhibit some obviously impractical knowledge was immediately denounced as a "doctor"—whether this referred to the medical profession, or was meant to accuse all nonwholesale merchants as potential Ph.D.'s, Berman never explained.) "You're killing me. Do you think if people really liked blank pages, *The Saturday Evening Post* would have anything else?"

The marketing department would nod wearily, and for the next advertisement they would be handicapped with a Berman catch-phrase to feature. One of these last stood on an easel between the director and his assistant:

YOUR GROCERIES TOIL
WHEN YOU SAVE ROYAL

it read, and several more choice examples adorned the peeling mustard-colored walls:

CAMERAS AND MINK COATS IN ALL DIFFERENT SIZES—
THESE ARE JUST SOME OF ROYAL PURPLE'S GREAT
PRIZES

THE ROYAL PURPLE MARK SHOULD BE YOUR SHOPPING
GUIDE
GET YOUR MONEY'S FULL WORTH AND THE PREMIUMS
BESIDE

A LITTLE BIRD SAYS "CHIRP,
YOU SHOULD SAVE WITH ROYAL PURP"

Bothered with declining redemptions and an increasing reluctance of newer stores to join the Royal Purple family, as Berman liked to call it, the marketing department began to strike back. Slowly the white space in their ads began spreading. Large photographs started to bleed off the page. Copy shrank to the point of invisibility. Class and tone won the day. The last full-page advertisement had been solid purple; a white marginal stripe ran from the upper right to the lower left, with, in the lower right, an imperial crest under the words "royal purple" in miniscule lower-case type.

"Mystique," said the Director of Marketing.

"Mystique, shmystique," screamed Berman, his hand pressed to his heart. "It's a mystery, that's what it is. A mystery why I'm not dead from aggravation. Five thousand dollars for two lousy words without even capital letters yet. Oh, oh, oh. I'm dying."

Nevertheless, the tide had slowly begun to turn.

Prosperity turned the corner. Royal Purple's salesmen, who looked like reformed protection racketeers and who were, for the most part, unreformed protection racketeers, began to encounter less difficulty in persuading storeowners to feature Royal Purple stamps. The immediate results were increasing sales, decreasing numbers of smashed windows, and Berman's good mood.

"Now that I've said good about you, it don't mean that I'm happy about some of those cockamamy notions. Understand, I think you're on the right track. You ain't pushcart hustlers like me, but now and then you need a good pushcart hustler, eh, boys?"

He smiled expansively, and they all chorused. "Yes, Mr. Berman," with the exception of the director. He said, "That's right, Mr. Berman."

"You bet your Jockey shorts it's right, and if they taught you any different at Columbia, you oughta get out and sell a little with the boys."

The Princeton man winced slightly, partly at being taken for a Columbia graduate (Berman equated Columbia with the higher classes, as opposed to City College and New York University), and partly at the thought of associating with Berman's staff of plug-ugly salesmen.

Berman almost felt a sense of fatherly pride in the young crew that stood before him. After all, the redemption centers were busy trading merchandise for stamps—good merchandise on which Royal Purple's cut amounted to something like twice retail less half wholesale. With every ring of thousands of cash registers, Sol Berman looked upon his employees with increasing fondness.

"Let me tell you a story, boys. Five years ago I said to my ex-partner, 'Hy,' I said, 'how can you go wrong? People have to eat, right? People have to wash their clothes, right? We have to make money, right? So you give them cigar coupons. It worked once, it'll damn well work again.' That's what they don't teach you doctors in college."

The marketing staff shuffled its feet at the mention of cigar coupons; one of the juniors began to pack up the presentation. Berman beamed.

"Don't let it go to your heads now, but you can tell your mothers I think you're doing good work." The director winced again. "You bleed a little and get an ulcer or two, and you'll know what it's like to get your feet wet in the business. You get second sense after a while, and I tell you, Purple coupons are going places. You listened to me," he concluded genially, "and now we're beginning to shape up."

The bedroom was the first room to fall before Lynn's determined onslaught. As her inquisitive broom swept back and forth below the bed, interesting treasures came to light. One was a complete Sunday *New York Times*, in all its five-pound sectioned glory, dated the previous November. Another item, however, contained more information in a smaller package—it was a wayward garter hook trailing a few forlorn threads at the point where it had once been joined to its dangling brothers and sisters.

This last item Lynn treated like a bedbug. Holding it distastefully between her forefinger and thumb, she deposited it hastily in the refuse, as if a picture of the old super, winking broadly, were in the back of her mind. Following quickly, George's appointment calendar, with its mysterious inscriptions and not-so-mysterious appointments, joined it.

When the job of straightening up the bedroom had been accomplished, she turned to the remainder of the apartment with all the determination of the *Hausfrau*. War was declared on each little tumbleweed of dust, every last cracker crumb in the sofa, until the final triumph of an unconditional annihilation would be achieved. (Anyone who doubts that the female of the species will inevitably take over the planet in a Thurberian war has never seen her, eyes aflame, pursuing to its doom a tumbleweed in a New York apartment.)

But overlaid on the predatory housekeeper was an aura of happiness. Lynn went slowly from chair to table, from bed to sofa—shifting, brushing, wiping, and dusting. Be it ever so humble, a voice might have been whispering to her, there's no place like a home—even if it's not yours. Her bare feet danced over the carpet; she showed such a proprietary interest in every slat of the venetian blinds that a casual observer would have pegged her as the part-owner of a cooperative, at least. The joy of becoming a member of a home, even for such a short time and on such a tentative basis, was awakening all sorts of dormant desires in the consciousness of this young girl. And one of them was to take a long bath.

One of the more disturbing things about the Place, Lynn had always found, was the absence of a bath—or of a shower, for that matter. Baths granted to her by friends were always rushed, unsatisfactory affairs accompanied by thoughts of imposition and self-consciousness. And the stores Sally rented like as not come only with a rusty shower stall in one corner to serve next to Godliness.

But at this moment, tired and streaked with honest grime, Lynn developed a satisfying plan for the rest of the afternoon. The focus of her plan was in George's bathroom—a large, gleaming white tub, with one of its faucets promisingly labeled "H."

Replacing the cleaning implements in the various cubbyholes that pass for closets in a Manhattan apartment, she looked approvingly at the order she had brought from chaos and then quickly undressed in George's bedroom. A full-length mirror inside the door held her interest and won her admiration for a moment before all thoughts of the Place, Sylvia**?, housecleaning, garters and the old super's wink were lost in a bellowing cascade of water that rushed over her legs and began to climb quickly up the sides of her body. All

thoughts vanished, save those of George and the faucet
marked "H."

And then the telephone rang.

Lynn sighed, wrapped herself in a completely inadequate towel (that still bore faintly, if she had known
where to look, George's Army serial number in one corner) and squished her way into the bedroom.

"George? Hello, George? This is Stuie. Hello?"

Lynn had a blank look on her face. She was obviously trying to identify the subliminal urge that had
caused her to answer a phone that was not, by any
stretch of the imagination, hers.

"I'm afraid you have the wrong number," she finally
said, and cut Stuie off neatly in the middle of a final
"Hell—?"

She walked back to the bathroom thoughtfully. Steam
had clouded the window and mirror; the atmosphere
had taken on the opacity of a foggy day in Piccadilly.
Lynn slid back into the soothing water, once more giving herself up to thoughts of George and George's
apartment.

"Sometimes I think I must be nuts," she murmured,
luxuriously stretching in the caldron.

"I can only hope it's all been for the best," said Sally to
George offhandedly. "Although, I suppose the past few
years have been enough to strain the spirit of adventure
in even a young girl. In Clayville she was bored, but at
least she got around. Here, what have I gotten her into?
This, for one thing."

This referred to the neat stacks of Royal Purple trading stamps that George was removing from the offset
press.

Everything was going perfectly. El Greco's unerring
eye for matching colors had provided a perfect blend of
inks, and his plates had razor-sharp images. Working at
a very low speed, the press began to spew out thousands
of trading stamps printed on ordinary legal-size bond
paper, of which George had found a plentiful supply in

the puppet house. The constant *tictac-toe, tictac-toe* of the machine was strangely soothing to him; he worked rhythmically and happily, trailing his fingers on the stack of white paper and constantly adjusting the speed and pressure as he watched the first color runs begin to fill up the tray. Sally watched him lifting the first stack out of the machine. He handled the wet sheets delicately so that they would not smudge.

Sally sat at one side of the room listening to the rhythm of the press and, occasionally, making the rounds of the curtained windows to check on the clearness of the coast.

"Of course, she seems to be happy—a lot happier since you've been around," she continued, glancing at George archly, "which is good. God knows, we have few enough exciting times, even if things are generally quiet and comfortable."

"Have you always lived in Alabama?" asked George, carefully loading another run into the press.

"Lynn has, but I was brought up in New York. I never could stand small-town life in the South—I suppose *any* small-town life would be just as bad. No privacy. Privacy is a great privilege in a place like that. The normal way of life consists of parties, kaffeeklatsches, hen sessions—you turn out regularly to witness every ratty, faintly cultural roadshow that comes your way. Like third-rate violinists, fifth-rate Broadway companies, and Mrs. Ratcliffe's annual showing of her crocheted landscapes."

"Sounds like fun," said George.

"Sure," said Sally, "for about two days. Then it begins to pall. A city is different. In a city, privacy is the rule, not the expection. If you want parties, friendship . . . anything, it takes an effort, which is as it should be. If you don't like the creep living next door, you can go twenty years without even saying hello to her in the elevator. In almost any place west of the Hudson and south of Coney Island that kind of business would get you the reputation of the local lunatic who was probably killing herself with cocaine or heroin. Besides," she added, "I could never stand Coca-Cola for breakfast."

"What about Lynn?"

"That's my fault, I guess. All through her life I used to tell her stories about New York, mostly to keep myself on an even keel. Dated stories about the Hippodrome and the building of Rockefeller Center and the Empire State Building—about the Ritz and the aquarium at the Battery. So we both grew up frustrated; when she graduated the local junior college, we packed up our belongings, pawned her father's belongings, and arrived at Penn Station on a steamy July afternoon four years ago."

"Lynn told me all about that. She seems to be in pretty good shape, considering."

"Considering we live like . . . well, gypsies?" They both laughed, but Sally turned serious immediately. "It's true, and I know it. We're neither here nor there. We live in rented stores during the winter and camp out in the Park during the summer. I'm not knocking it, mind you. I'm just pointing out that it's all pretty uncertain, at its best. When things are good, they're very good. It's damn comfortable, and Lynn has plenty of good times. Sometimes I envy her. During the winter I see her dress up for dates and I know that she's off to one of the places I used to tell her about on those deadly long evenings in Clayville. But when she's down, she's a lot farther down than she ever used to be. I wish I knew where it would end. For me, it doesn't much matter. For Lynn, it's very important."

George stopped the press and lifted out the next pile of half-finished stamps. Sally made the rounds of the windows once more, peering intently out between the curtains on each wall. They were both intent on their moods of the moment: the man on the mechanical work which could destroy, for a short while, the little bug of uncertainty that was always crawling across his mind; the woman on an attempt to describe her way of life to a comparative stranger, and to herself.

"I suppose Lynn must be a pretty popular girl," said George.

"What does that mean? Popular with whom? She goes out a lot in season, but I don't know if you can imagine the people we are close to. Some aren't bad, but I wouldn't give a Confederate bill for the rest. Now, you I might consider as an eligible, if only I knew who or what you are."

"Does it make that much of a difference?" The press started its slow *tictac-toe tictac-toe* again.

"You're damn right it makes a difference. I'll give you five to three that as soon as you know that you're really George Smith, stockbroker, or George Jones, assistant to the vice-president, you'll be out of here so fast that you'll leave a permanent blur down Central Park West. You're a nice guy, but I don't think that once all the screws are assembled, Lynn will really seem to be your type."

"What's *her* type?"

"That's for her to tell you. Look, George. I know you're getting on fine, and I know Lynn has been in better shape than she's been in weeks. But she's very young, and she's been living a dream life on the surface of things for a long time. I wouldn't like to see her get hurt on the first descent. I don't know you. Lynn doesn't know you. For God's sake, you don't even know yourself. When that little old memory comes sneaking back one night, I think it might be a good idea for you to sneak back home with it. It might be better all around."

"Meanwhile?"

"Oh, hell," sighed Sally. "Meanwhile, stick around and make us some money. Someday Freddy and I are going to pack up and retire someplace outside the city—as soon as we can afford it and Lynn is settled by herself. Until then, Mercedes and Carmen remain at your service. Would you like the bumps on your head examined?"

"No thanks," said George with a grin. "The swelling's gone down, but you might still get a false reading."

"It's your nickel," Sally said. "Just be good to her, and leave quietly. No dramatics. It'll be the best way." She looked at her watch and then out the window. "I wonder what's keeping her?"

George drew a third run out of the press and stacked it carefully next to the other two. "I can let these dry overnight at the Place," he said. "I'll be ready to run the purple tomorrow. She said she'd be here."

"It's late," said Sally. "She should have been here by now."

Reluctantly Lynn stepped into her shoes and looked around the apartment. Everthing was tidy and clean— the bathroom had been scrubbed; the odds and ends of her lunch had been collected and deposited in one of the three paper bags she was going to take downstairs to the ashcans. She sat down at the desk and for the seventh or eighth time that afternoon picked up the heavy metal weight with his name on it. She would open her purse, and start to drop it in—then she would change her mind and set it down on the blotter again.

ƎЯƎVƎЯ ƎႸЯOƎႧ. It stood in front of her, returning her stare almost mockingly. ƎЯƎVƎЯ ƎႧЯOƎႧ.

She picked it up once more and began to open her purse. For a long minute she sat motionless, staring at the paperweight, at her purse, and into space. Then, with a decisive movement, she set it down on the desk once more, closing her purse with a snap.

ƎႧЯOƎႧ   would remain in the apartment. Instead she drew out a sheet of his notepaper and a pen. Carefully, underneath his address, she wrote: *I love you, George Revere,* and she signed it *Carman Gitana* with a flourish.

Gathering up the paper bags, Lynn began to make her way out of the house. She glanced for a moment at the sheet of paper lying on the desk and suddenly strode back into the living room, crumpled the message, and dropped it in the wastebasket underneath. Then, taking a last look around the quiet rooms, she stepped out into the hall and locked the door behind her.

"Throwing out the garbage, eh?"

Lynn started, nearly dropping one of the bags. The old super stood on the steps below her, grinning up from the shadows.

"Glad to see he's got someone to fix up for him. My old lady says he brought the roaches with him, and I wouldn't be a bit surprised."

"I didn't see a single bug," said Lynn hotly, surprised at her own anger.

"That so? Well, anyway, let me help you down."

"I can manage." Lynn climbed carefully down the steep, carpeted steps, the old man keeping a little way in front of her. They walked out through the hall in silence; he held the lid of a can while Lynn disposed of the spoils of her morning's cleaning, including George's appointment calendar and two crowded address books.

"Revere coming back soon?" asked the super conversationally, replacing the lid.

"I don't know," said Lynn. "I don't really know."

"Stood you up, eh?"

Lynn started to walk off down the street toward the Park.

"He's been ill," she said. "He'll be staying with a— with friends for a while."

"Hope he gets better soon," the old man called after her, but there was no answer.

How Sally and Lynn Went Shopping and There Was a Party

The past few days had been idyllic. George considered them the happiest of his life; although this may not have seemed to be a particularly notable cachet, considering the state of his memory, it was sufficient to put him in an extremely rosy mood. He explored the Park with Lynn, from the almost impenetrable Bramble in the north, with its thickets of nesting birds, to the incredible variety of monuments and statuary in the south; from the model boat races in the east to The Pool and the rolling hills of the west. They tramped around the reservoir, climbed to the Fort Clinton blockhouse, ran through the Gardens, and lay under towering trees whose fluttering leaves filtered the sun's bright disk into a million flashing pinpoints of brilliant light.

Two things alone kept intruding into his new sense of himself. Sally's words of a few days before kept popping into his thoughts at the most unexpected places and times. He would find himself looking at Lynn and thinking of what she might look like to George Smith or George Jones. Would George Smith be fascinated by the faded, threadbare Levis, or would he be repelled by anything that didn't smack of Norell or Balenciaga? Would George Jones fall head over heels for the blond straggly hair, scattered by the winds into a thousand forms and fringes, or would he shrink from any hirsute arrangement not officially sanctioned by Mr. Kenneth? Would George Brown be willing to give his heart to the product of the seasons, or the product of Max Factor;

to the creation of Miss Finch and Bennington, or the creation of Clayville J.C. and Central Park?

And Lynn had not helped by falling into sudden, unpredictable fits of moodiness—as dark and short-lived as the black summer stormclouds that occasionally rode high over the island. Was she thinking the same thoughts? She would refuse to discuss it, suddenly leaping to her feet and racing through some startled baseball team's left field, leading George on a zigzag race that would end, stumblingly and breathlessly, in a cool, green, mossy clearing where the roar of autos and busses cutting through the Park roadways muted to a distant, pleasant swishing—the rote at a deserted coast.

George now walked slowly up the path to the Tower, two hundred thousand Royal Purple stamps—a fifth of his week's output—in a bulky brown paper sack under his arm. Behind him, the puppet house was clean and deserted; the offset press stood silent and secretive.

He looked around, circling aimlessly near the steps until there were no passersby in the immediate vicinity. Then he knocked the five rhythmical knocks ("shave and a haircut") as Lynn had shown him; an eye immediately appeared in a small hole in the boarded and blacked-out window. Lynn let him in and closed the door behind him.

The room was reasonably well lit by four of the battery-operated emergency lamps that hung from the ceiling. An informal assembly line had been arranged, and it was humming.

In front of the door was a stack of trading stamps sitting in the middle of a litter of crumpled wastepaper, discards, and confetti. At this station Lynn was going through the output, sheet by sheet, weeding out the blanks, bad registrations, inverts, and smudged copies. Once the good sheets had been separated, the perforating began. El Greco had lent them his automatic perforator—a fifteen-inch segment of a dead branch through which over two hundred wire brads had been driven in

more or less a straight line. With this instrument, and
with a slab from an old automobile tire as backing,
Lynn was punching the rows of holes between stamps in
a highly professional manner.

Beyond this pile of litter, Sally sat cross-legged on the
floor, cutting the sheets into strips with an expression of
ferocious concentration and a pair of large, wicked-look-
ing shears. Each time a sheet had been reduced to fourteen strips, she further reduced the strips to groups of
varying sizes—from singles to complete rows. These she
then threw into a shopping bag, where she constantly
mixed them up by joggling the bag or by stirring them
with her hand. "Double, double, toil and trouble," she
had started saying some days before, but had long since
given it up in the face of a noticeably reduced apprecia-
tiveness on the part of her fellow workers. Occasionally
she would also bring her hand out of the shopping bag
with the bright announcement, "Ladies and Gentlemen:
the next number is H-7—H-7, ladies and gentlemen!",
but this was getting just as poor a reception and she
eventually dropped it, too.

End man on the line was Freddy. Freddy sat at the
table surrounded by bottles of glue, blank stamp books,
and gloom. He complained to anyone who would listen
that all the fingers of his left hand were now completely
glued together and that it was only a matter of time before his right hand joined them, figuratively and liter-
ally. Sally had persuaded him to wear an apron, but
small pieces of paper were stuck to all parts of his
hands, arms, and face, testifying to places where blobs
of glue had found a home. In the midst of this sorry
scene, he was pulling handfuls of stamps out of Sally's
shopping bag and sticking them down at random in the
books. A pile of finished products—sixty-five bulging
books at the moment—stood at the far end of the table.

"Well, this is the last of it," said George brightly. He
received no answer other than a groan from Sally and a
hostile stare from Freddy, who had just discovered that
one of his eyelids had become glued open.

"Store these in the corner with the rest of our nest egg," he instructed Lynn, giving her the package. "I'll take over inspection and perforation for a while." He sat down and began wielding Greco's hole-puncher. Lynn moved beside him and continued shuffling through the papers, looking for irregular prints.

After a while George broke into the buzz of activity "I suppose we might as well plan for tomorrow," he said, to everyone and no one in particular, "since we'll probably be through with this first batch before noon."

"How many books will we have altogether?" asked Sally.

"Oh, a hundred or so."

"Let's see. Freddy, what has been our best bet in photographic equipment?"

Freddy thought for a while. "Most good stuff they'll take in the pawn shops runs twenty, thirty books," he said. "If George and I are going to do the hocking in one trip, we should get two sets of equipment that won't look too funny being pledged."

"How about a couple of movie cameras and a couple of projectors," suggested George.

"Might do it," said Freddy. "No. Come to think of it, the redemption outfits might get curious if two sets went out at the same time. I think we'll pick up one set of still equipment—say, a thirty-five millimeter job, a slide projector, and some accessories—and a set of movie stuff—a camera, a projector. I'll check the catalog to make sure there are no special orders there."

"That sounds fair enough," said George. "Let's leave it this way, then. The girls will take about fifty books each, depending on Freddy's calculations. You'll go to different redemption centers, of course. Lynn, you take care of the slide equipment. You'll get the camera, projector, maybe a screen or a flash attachment—whatever you need to fill out the fifty books without waiting for special orders. Sally, you can handle the movie equipment. Same thing. You'll both bring the stuff back here, and Freddy and I will take them around to Third Avenue and pawn them. Let's say I'll take the movie, and Freddy the still."

"Suppose they're all out?" asked Lynn.

"Anything you can get in the way of photographic equipment," said Freddy, "but try not to move into Sally's area. We don't want them to start checking with one another."

"Right," said Sally. "And if there's no photo stuff, we go back to musical instruments."

"We should have more of a plan than that," said George, taking charge. "OK, here goes. Lynn, if you can't fill in on still-photo equipment, switch to anything in the general area of entertainment machines.

"Entertainment machines?"

"Radios, TVs, tape recorders, stereo phonographs—that kind. And Sally, if *you* run into trouble in the movie end, you switch to do-it-yourself-type things."

"Tools?"

"If necessary. But I was thinking more in the line of typewriters, musical instruments—maybe expensive sports equipment, like golf clubs. Power tools are a last resort."

"Hey," said Freddy, "where did you learn so much about hock shops?"

"You get around, you learn," said George, looking at Lynn.

"How much do you think we'll get out of all this?" she asked.

"Your mother and I figured about a hundred dollars would be a good bet," answered George. "If it goes off smoothly, we can really start going."

"*Really* start going?" Freddy cried in anguish. "As it is, I'm going to have to spend a day at the public baths just to get the glue off."

"It's up to Sally," said George. "We've got enough of a backlog to keep us going for weeks, and I can make as many more stamps as anybody wants."

Sally was quiet. "I suppose the more the better," she finally said, "but we really don't need to make this a full-time job. After all, the plates will still be here next summer, and we're in pretty good shape at the moment."

"But, Mother," interrupted Lynn. "It's almost the end of the season already. Shouldn't we do all we can now?"

"That's right, too. Well, let's say we'll print as many more as we can, but we'll only process them like this," and she swept her hand around the busy room, "as we need them. Perhaps, every other weekend or so, we'll knock out a couple of hundred dollars' worth for the hell of it."

Freddy was appalled. "You mean we gotta go through this every other week? After a while my clothes'll get glued to my skin and I'll never be able to take them off again."

"It's rough making an honest living," agreed Sally.

They worked on through the afternoon: George and Lynn inspecting and punching, Sally cutting and shuffling, Freddy pasting and complaining. Shortly after six, one pair of lamps abruptly dimmed. Freddy jumped up and turned it off.

"I think this battery had just about had it," he said. "I recharged it last night, but I guess it's just getting old. They don't make automobiles the way they used to."

"We'd better call it quits, then," said Sally. "I'll need whatever juice is left to start dinner going—the lights won't be coming on until late."

"Better hold off," suggested Freddy. "This one's just about dead, and I don't know how long the other will keep the burners going. We'll think about getting a new battery tomorrow."

"Dinner at nine, then," Sally announced. "The factory is adjourned until then."

They all stood and stretched. George and Lynn left the Place and walked down the hill toward the outdoor theater. They walked quietly, hand in hand, melting into the hundreds of couples who had been promenading back and forth over their heads for the past few hours.

"Why so thoughtful?" asked George.

Lynn seemed to have sunk abruptly into one of her moods. She squeezed his hand briefly.

"Nothing," she said. "I was trying to think of a good last name for you."

"How about Harmony?" suggested George.

Lynn laughed shortly. "No fun in that. I would like . . ." She left the sentence trailing and then finished it in another direction. "I think George is fine, after all."

"George George?"

"No," she smiled. "One is plenty."

They crossed the bridle path and began to wander along the steep glades near Central Park West. The sky began to take on a deeper shade of blue. The sun hung low over the wall of apartment houses like an orange; in the distance, the Fifth Avenue windows glittered back at it. A large electric sign shouted "Hampshire House, Hampshire House" over and over again to the unheeding trees and lakes below.

They sat behind a row of hedges that separated them from a long grassy slope on which a comfortable family group—busy mother, sleeping father, and three shouting children—guarded the remains of a picnic lunch. Past them a group of teen-agers tirelessly coasted their bikes from the top of the slope to the bottom and then, just as tirelessly, climbed back to their starting place again.

George stretched out on the grass, feeling the first dampness of the evening dew through his thin slacks. He lowered his head into Lynn's lap and looked up at her chin.

She was staring straight ahead—into the middle of tomorrow or yesterday, it seemed to George. She did not look down at him until he raised his hand and held it alongside her cheek. Then she smiled.

"Penny for your thoughts," he said.

Lynn turned serious for a moment. "They'll cost you

a great deal more than that," she said.

They sat there, like that, until the park lights went on. "Dinnertime," said Lynn. He kissed her and they made their way, slowly, back to the Place.

Montage: The assembly line in operation again. Freddy, triumphantly, holding the last stamp. Extreme close-up of the stamp being pasted in the book. Last-minute instructions. Exterior shot of Sally and Lynn on their way into the outside world. Shots of busses, automobiles, traffic lights turning red and green, crowds crossing street. Closeup of George and Freddy biting their nails. Clock ticking off minutes. Full shots of Royal Purple Trading Stamp Gift Centers. Cut from Sally to Lynn, entering. They talk to understanding clerks. Split screen. Matte simultaneous scenes in the two centers. Lynn gets her equipment. Sally substitutes a tape recorder for a camera. Insert shots of two projectors going into shopping bags. Close-up of stamp books changing hands.

Dissolve to telescopic long shot of Sally and Lynn meeting on Columbus Circle. Dolly through the Park. Cut to George and Freddy, still waiting. Clock ticking off minutes. Insert pile of fingernails at their feet. Door opens. Reunion. Shopping bags change hands and the men leave.

Process shot and special effects. Freddy and George walking against background of three brass balls. Traffic montage again. Insert medium close shot of bells jingling as a door opens. Split screen showing Freddy and George greeting pawnbrokers and placing merchandise on counter. Pan items: a movie projector, an editor, a tape recorder, thirty-five-millimeter camera, a slide projector, and a projection screen. Close-up, split screen, of proprietors' faces showing extreme interest. Cut to medium close shot of Lynn and Sally, biting their nails. Insert clock, ticking minutes away. Close shot of pile of fingernails still growing. Dissolve.

Special-effects shot of money showering down: fives,

tens, twenties. Montage: Smiling faces of the pawnbrokers, George, and Freddy; jangling bells; three brass balls; traffic shots. Exterior long shot of George and Freddy meeting near the Plaza. Insert of a pawn ticket changing hands. Dolly with Freddy as he leaves George and walks into a hotel around the corner. Medium shot of Freddy waiting in lobby. Insert close-up of elevator indicator needle coming down to "Main." Doors open. Freddy engages in conversation with elevator man. Cutaway to elevator man's head, nodding. Insert two pawn tickets changing hands. Repeat special-effects shot of money showering down.

Dissolve to dolly shot of Freddy and George walking through the Park, singing and talking. Cut to girls, still waiting. They are sitting in a pile of fingernails that reaches to their knees. Insert clock: big hand on four, little hand on twelve. Close-up of knuckles on door. Interior. George and Freddy walk in. Reunion. Close shot of table. Repeat for the third time special-effects shot of money showering down. (Note: this screen adaptation had been slanted toward a low-budget production.) Close pan of faces: George, smiling; Freddy, joyous; Lynn, flabbergasted; Sally, incredulous.

Insert title: "One Hundred and Seventy-five Dollars! Good God!"

Fade out.

George closed the door of the Place behind him and walked thoughtfully out into the late-afternoon sunlight. Behind him, behind the old door, an impromptu party was in progress. In one corner Sally and Freddy were arranging and rearranging the bills into different piles as they talked excitedly about the possibility of saving enough to retire. Freddy had forgotten his misery at being soaked in glue for five days, while Sally was having second thoughts about her determination not to go too far too fast in the printing business. At the other end of the room Lynn was engaged in an excited and animated conversation with El Greco; the painter had been torn away from his Whistler to share in the makeshift cold-cuts buffet that had been brought from a nearby delicatessen.

George had wandered back and forth between the two conversations for a while, joining neither and feeling very alone all at once.

"And so, my child, I tell him that choosing a painting is like choosing a wife—you can flirt all you want with the fashionable prostitutes, but a wife you have to *live* with, no? So he says I am a fifth-rate artist. 'A fifth-rate artist?' I say. 'A fifth-rate artist is twice as good as a first-rate dealer!' Good, eh? They treat paintings like wallpaper, yes?"

"It's a lot of money, but do we really need to keep going all the time? After all, we have enough to keep up through the winter. Should it be anything more than mad money? Perhaps we'll have a good season and we can make enough legitimately to call it quits."

"But the paintings I like are the ones that show the world at its best—bright and green, singing. That one with millions and millions of lilies floating out of the canvas into the air—you can feel the morning mist across the years of that man's garden. Even here, you can see the mist that comes out of The Lake at dawn. It's a different world. Sometimes I wish I didn't have to go back."

"First, of course, we'll have to make sure the land has never been sprayed. DDT can last for years and years, and arsenic forever. It's a crime. We'll clear the land ourselves, if necessary, to get good dirt like we have here. Then mulch—lots of it—and manure." Freddy looked up and saw George standing idly at the periphery of their animated conversation. Sally looked up at the same time. "Oh, George," she said, "Freddy and I thought we'd get another auto battery tonight so we can finish out the season with light in here. We'll leave at eleven, and Freddy will brief you on the way. Feel up to it?"

George grinned weakly. "Why not? If Lynn's description of the procedure is up to date, it might be fun."

"It is and it will be," promised Sally, turning back to Freddy and their interrupted plans.

Munching a strip of corned beef, George strolled irresolutely around the cavernous room once or twice and finally slipped outside. Only Lynn saw him go. She rose to her feet for a moment, but something Greco had just said claimed her interest, and then the moment had passed. She sat down again.

George moved slowly along the twisting footpaths that led south through the center of the Park. He skirted the Lake, where the first of the nine-to-fivers were beginning to assert themselves on the lines awaiting rowboats. The path was sticky from the day's accumulation of chocolate custard that had flowed through holes in cones and around stickly fingers, to come to rest underfoot.

He walked on mechanically and deliberately, past the last bend of the Lake, past the incredible Belvedere Fountain—its layer-cake tiers splashing water down to cover the ankles of two or three delighted children below. He passed through the dank vault leading to the Mall, listening to each footstep echoing bleakly from the stone walls and the grimy tile mosaics on the dim arch of the roof. He climbed to a point overlooking the bandshell, deserted now and facing scattered rows of empty benches. There was a small flower-covered arched pagoda there; he sat under it, on a small wooden bench, staring at the memory (or was it the prophecy?) of a thousand *Capriccio Italiens* and *Carnivals of Venice* below him.

How much longer could he keep the pretense up? *How much longer,* he kept thinking, *can I kid myself that a man can keep going without an identity, without a home, with just his wits and a dream?* How long could he live in New York, tilting at windmills, before ending up on a street corner with the others who seemed to share his desperate apartness? How long, finally, did he really want to stay away from those norms that are dictated so strongly by protective aunts and frightened mothers that he could remember them now, although of himself he could remember nothing? Nine to five. White shirt and a tie. Stand straight. Brush your teeth twice a day. Drink your milk. Think. Laugh at the boss's jokes. Shine your shoes. Get it wholesale. Smile. Ask for a raise. Get married. Straighten your socks. Put away your clothes. Smile.

He tried very hard to sort out the facts of the past week from the fancies, but he would always come back to an unconcealable salience: he, George Something, was becoming the criminal leader of an unlikely gang of lunatics and bums in the middle of the most highly organized society in the world—Manhattan Island.

"George Something, interviewed in his forest hideway off Eighty-fifth Street, said to our reporter that he would not stop his raids on the middle classes until they had returned all of their hostages to freedom."

I could give myself up to the Bureau of Missing Persons, he thought. *I could walk up to them and say, "I'm missing. I've lost myself and you can find me. I think I've been in the Army, so you could probably trace my fingerprints. Or maybe trace this key through a locksmith. Or look for laundry marks in my underwear. Or publish my picture in the papers with a reward for the best identification. Can you do it?"*

Of course they could. But could he? And would he return across the bridle path one day, bringing an identity to the foot of the Tower—to Lynn? Or would it become a dream? Is it, was it, will it be—a dream?

"Hi."

George looked quickly around. A stranger had joined him on the bench—a dapper young man with a tousled mass of hair over an extremely graceful face, a heavy silver chain around his neck, and a pair of trousers so tight they appeared to be wrapped, like puttees, around his legs.

"Doing anything tonight, sweetheart?"

"I'm a cop," said George and watched the tight trousers moving quickly down the path like two runaway mailing tubes. With a sigh he arose and resumed his stroll down the Mall.

The sky was beginning to dim; the occupants of the benches had started squinting at their newspapers in order to squeeze the last drop of bad news and tragedy from the dying sun. George moved on, kicking at an occasional pebble, thinking of each of them in turn. He tried to imagine why they didn't return home after the day's work was finished. He pictured them without an identity, like himself—would they have been so calm, so content? An old man was spreading wet bread for the pigeons: he took each crust, dampened it in a coffee can full of water on the bench beside him, pulled the dough apart in his fingers, and dropped the pieces to the sidewalk, where twenty or thirty birds ran to fight briefly over each new treasure. What was his home—a tired daughter and hostile son-in-law? Probably, and the pigeons would wind up someday under glass in a West Side restaurant serviced by Freddy and his friends.

The Mall gave way to an asphalt roadway, and the dimness of late afternoon gave way to the dusk of early evening. George moved through the endless rows of benches, until all at once he found himself staring at a pair of eyes that stared back incredulously. He looked at the man, feeling a fluttering chill of recognition begin in the small of his neck and flash out to his fingertips and his brain. He reached out to grasp it, to trap it, even as he saw the man's mouth open and heard, in a crescendo of sensations:

"Hey, George. George Revere. Where the hell have you been?"

7 *How George Took a Walk*

George Revere sat on the edge of his bed and hated his typewriter. It was not general hostility, but hatred of each specific part of the machine that was not helping to make the almost blank page any less blank. He hated the *q*, the *w*, the *e*, and the *r;* he hated *a,s,d,* and *f.* He hated *zxcvbnm,* the periods and the commas. He hated all the numbers. He hated # and @. In a moment of irrational loathing, he even hated the shift keys.

The play had stunk. Even Sylvia had noticed that, and George found a minimum of comfort in blaming her precipitous departure on the wretchedness of the evening's entertainment.

"It'll only take me forty-five minutes to bat out a review," he had pleaded. "We can be back to my apartment by twelve-thirty. The show wasn't that bad."

"Lousy," Sylvia had hissed.

"Oh, I don't know. I grant that it was a pretty loose production and probably not at all in keeping . . . "

That was when Sylvia had observed that it had stunk.

"That's unfair."

"Unfair, hell. I suppose that's what you'll write in your little column: 'It was a loose production' or something. Well, it stunk."

"OK, so it wasn't *Death of a Salesman.* Let's have a drink and talk it over."

But Sylvia had trotted down the long flight of stairs into the subway leaving George to return to the *Alarum* office, alone, and later, still alone, to his apartment.

The sheet of paper in his typewriter was headed

DETROIT, DETROIT!
by
George Revere

and it was curled around the roller in a nearly permanent bend, in protest against having been flattened into the machine for months. In a wave of excess creativity, which was probably more than three-quarters frustration, George had disinterred what was to be his first novel and was trying, once again, to unlock the jumbled puzzle of his thoughts. The Muse had come upon him suddenly as he was brushing his teeth, and had then tantalizingly slipped out of his grasp. Dressed only in his undershorts, he sat on the unmade bed, crushing the edge of his mattress out of shape, and scowled at the typewriter.

It had all seemed so easy. Books were being written every day about growing up: growing up in New York, in Boston, in Chicago, in Skully's Landing, Mississippi. Even growing up in Asheville, North Carolina. George had grown up in Detroit, and as he sat facing the empty page, the scenes, the incidents, the colors, and the voices came back to him—disordered, fugitive, and real. He had been trying desperately to transfer the Detroit he remembered from the corners of his mind to the keyboard in front of him. Where to start? Why not the smell of roasting apples and marshmallows, eaten on sticky coathangers in front of the roaring autumn-leaf bonfires on Yorkshire? Or the Sunday excursions to Bob-Lo: the four-decker streamer leaving from the Vernor's Ginger Ale plant in a flurry of churning water and band music?

But George could no more shape a framework for his story, or even for his life, out of the quick succession of shifting scenes than he could understand how the same types of thoughts, the same types of experiences, could have nourished a generation of writers.

Each scene remained with him like a shiny Christmas-tree ornament, but they hung in midair. There was no tree.

The visions washed over George in waves, and the typewriter keyboard stared through them, silent, malevolent. The roller coaster at Eastwood Park. Saturday-afternoon serials at the Harper or the Alger (*The Black Whip*. He had almost forgotten *The Black Whip*), and the tragedy when admission went from nine to ten cents. The forest hideouts down the middle of Chandler Park Drive and the vacant-lot tree houses. The P-40 and Stuka models at the bike shop. And helping to paddle the big wood-and-canvas canoe, with the built-in morning-gloryhorn Victrola, through the quiet sun-sparkled canals of Belle Isle. (The canoe, the Victrola, the paddle—all gone in the sudden and unbelievable boathouse fire.)

Suddenly George felt cold. It was not an eerie chill or a psychic frost—just cold. From the window a whirring air-conditioner was raining huge quantities of cold, electric-smelling air onto him like an invisible cold shower. He was reaching for his trousers, which hung over the arm of a chair, when the telephone rang.

As he pulled the instrument toward him, his paper-weight, a linotype slug with GEORGE REVERE set in sixty-point Franklin Gothic Condensed Roman, crashed to the floor, catching the end of his big toe. George swore and kicked at it in annoyance. It didn't move far. George swore again.

"Hello? Yeah, hello, Stuie. No, no, not at all. No, really. Sylvia? Well, she—No, she's fine. Aren't you, Sylvia? What? The review should be there. Sure, I gave it to Pete. Did you check Conklin's desk? Oh. Yeah, I'm sure it'll be there. Look, Stuie, are you going to cut me under twenty inches again? I know it was a lousy show, but Kerr and Watts get plenty of room to be nasty in. Why not me? Oh. Oh. Yeah, well, it's up to you, Stuie. If you can see it in your heart to cut into Dick's review of *The Son of the Ten Commandments* or whatever, I'd appreciate at least twenty . . . What?

Yeah. Sylvia, Stuie says hello. She says hello back, Stuie. No, you didn't. I know, I know. I'll be seeing you. Good-bye, Stuie. Yeah, so long."

By the time George hung up the receiver, he had wriggled into his trousers, and the momentum had carried him into his shoes and a faded green short-sleeved shirt that had been lying at the foot of the bed. He stood at the door of the bedroom for a moment, tightening his belt and scowled at the typewriter. Somehow, the moment for *Detroit, Detroit!* had passed. George switched off the light and let himself out of the apartment. There was a bright half-moon overhead, whitening the sidewalk, and the heat hung over the city like an Afghan rug. George began walking toward Central Park.

The problem with George, oddly enough, was Success. Not SUCCESS spelled out in ruby-inset gold letters, blinking on and off in the glare of diamond-encrusted Klieg lights. Not at all. George's Success was mostly lowercase, spelled out in adequate paychecks and a profession where quiet nondescript men move through the ruby-and-diamond brilliance of SUCCESS and, once in a while, leave a calling card at the rear entrance.

The iron curtain between capital-S Success and SUCCESS did not separate the men from the boys; it separated complacency from melodrama, and George was a lousy actor.

He had landed in the *Alarum* mailroom fresh from two years of fighting the peace with a mimeograph at Fort Benning, Georgia. At twenty-four, as he operated the mailroom's small presses, George had refused to admit to himself that he did not want to scale the heights, bachelor's degree in hand and his editorship of a college literary magazine as a shield. Had he been willing to admit that he liked operating the mailroom printing equipment, he might still be there, a lowercase success quietly enjoying himself. But he was young, and he had heard that to be young was to be ambitious. Ergo, a capital-S Success and the frustration of the iron curtain as reward.

George had been graduated from the University of Michigan, class of 1957, with an arts degree, a working knowledge of Shakespeare and Salinger, a Phi Beta Kappa key, and a general sense that the world was Ann Arbor squared—a vast campus in which one can drink beer, write learned essays on subjects of no interest to oneself or one's professor, and be rewarded with scholarship money and a daily schedule. Oddly enough, he was not too wrong. Fort Benning had been Ann Arbor with uniforms.

George had thoroughly enjoyed his two years in the U.S. Army Combat Mimeograph Corps, or whatever it had been called. He liked the machines, and he liked the smell of ink as it sloshed around in the whirling tanks all day. He loved his job in the *Alarum* mailroom, too. He had been told the mailroom was supposed to be the first step in becoming a reporter, perhaps; but he loved the mimeographs, the dittos, the offsets—seven whirling, clanking machines voraciously gulping down sheets of white bond paper, one at a time, and spewing out multicolored gems of the printer's art. George liked to walk through the print shop—twiddling a dial here, adding some ink there, relaxing the paper-feed-spring tension at one place, and raising an upper margin a sixteenth of an inch at another. He loved laying out the procedures manuals, planning the four-color announcements for the Bowling Club. And he was not ready when the nod came that sent him into the makeup department.

Slowly he had left the smell of ink and the chug of the small presses and had progressed his way up into the maze of the organization, until he had reached his present vantage point on the City Desk, with occasional assignments as third-string drama critic covering off-off-Broadway, with its endless revivals of Shakespeare, Gilbert and Sullivan, and Strindberg. It was the knothole

through which he could see the Kliegs of SUCCESS on
the other side of the curtain, but his heart was with the
pounding presses and the clattering linotype machines
in the basement—the pulsing muscle of the *Alarum* that
he saw only at infrequent times when an emergency
called him down to change a last-minute head.

George swung on through the darkness, reflecting on
his new career. It was not that he did not like the
thought of climbing the ladder of success, as the publisher of the *Alarum* was always saying. (It was a particularly unfortunate simile, which always made George
think of ascending, like a fireman, into a burning building.) It was just that George rather liked the idea of
printing, and also rather hated the theater.

George's ideas about the theater were twofold. First,
his attachment to the printed page (an attachment fos-
tered by college, where his reverence for the drama was
carefully limited to heavily footnoted editions; and possi-
bly heightened by his work with the mailroom presses)
precluded any understanding of the spoken word as an
art form. It was doubtful if he could ever really understand why a group of adults would play "Let's Pretend"
for two hours, while another group of people, no less
idiotically, would pay $9.90 for the privilege of watch-
ing them. Most of George's distaste for this phenomenon could probably be traced to the shows he had been
called on to review over the past two years: being well
off the beaten track, they were generally presented in
the vestry-rooms of abandoned churches by casts continually embarrassed at outnumbering their audiences.
Years of reviewing experimental productions had left
George with an uncomfortable feeling that the theater
was the result of compulsive exhibitionism, and viewing
a play was not unlike the experience he had once had of
watching a tanked-up young lady undressing in a Sixth
Avenue bar—it was a feeling compounded of equal
parts interest, embarrassment, curiosity, and (as in the
case of the young lady, who was hustled off in a paddy

wagon at a premature moment in her act) disappointment.

George's second fixation about the theater was makeup. Sitting almost in the laps of the actors night after night gradually replaced all sense of drama in his soul with a fascination about theatrical cosmetics. He could remember every plastic ridge, putty seam, false eyelash, and grain of powder in a long-gone play of which he could not even recall the title. A juvenile with a suntan, bleeding Max Factor No. 2 all over the collar of his shirt, could successfully keep George's attention from the plot for two acts. And the appearance of a skin wig, betrayed by a bumpy cranial dome and a forehead crease that disappeared behind the ears, would enchant him for an entire evening.

Needless to say, this last preoccupation had nearly lost George his assignments on several occasions. He was sure that a few more telltale reviews bearing the stamp of an unmistakable monomania would render him *persona non grata* in the drama section. But he still frequently found the temptation to write that "Miss So-and-So, scattering face powder from every Scotch-taped wrinkle, delivered her lines as if she were afraid that they would adhere to her gummy lipstick." He also carried this awareness over into his daily life. He would speculate on the heavy spot of pancake under Sylvia's left eye—a blemish? a mole? a crow's-foot? He could contemplate for hours the minute, almost unnoticeable gestures Ginny (Miss Drainola, 1965) would make as she attempted to keep a false eyelash from falling off.

But most frustrating of all were the nights, like tonight, when the assistant critic could not manage to take over an opening on Broadway from the chief sitter, and George would find himself behind a lady in a hairdo larger than a Garbo hat, among people he did not know, and who, moreover, had no interest in knowing him. Once in a while a critic from another paper would ask him for a pencil, but generally they let him alone.

And this play, as Sylvia had so neatly observed, had stunk. Still, that was no reason for her to—

George would never be able to put the next scene together properly, although he would try for a long while before giving up. First, someone shouted his name from the head of the path—it was an agonized scream, as if his nameless friend were trying to warn him of an approaching terror. He stopped short and suddenly heard a rustling in the bushes just behind him. He turned quickly, just as something heavy and hard caught him on the side of his head.

A kaleidoscope flashed and whirled in his brain; for one beautiful moment, he was back at his typewriter and everything was going fine . . . and going fine . . . and going fine . . .

And then everything went.

8 How Stuie Ross Smelled a Rat and Herman Saw a Gorilla

"Hey, George. George Revere. Where the hell have you been?"

George stood stone-still for an everlasting split second, gaping witlessly at the man who had bounded off the bench and was striding toward him. The fluttering thing was close now, so close that he tried to clear his mind completely for its coming. *I've got it,* he thought over and over again. *I've got it.* Like a butterfly collector inching stealthily through the whispering grass with his net poised to trap, in an instant of time, the darting evanescent shape he has long sought, George's mind was teetering on a knife edge of uncertainty. Then suddenly, with a calm finality that left his knees a little weak and his stomach clutched in a damp knot, he knew.

"Stuie," he said wonderingly. "It's Stuie Ross."

"You were expecting maybe Mrs. Nussbaum?" Ross boomed heartily. "So where have you been? You look a little green, there, old man. Not at all like a guy who's been on a week's vacation. Come to think of it, you look more like you've been on a week's bat. How about it?"

"I'm all right, Stuie. I just felt a little . . . odd, there, for a second."

"Odd? Conklin should hear you say you feel odd. He'd probably heave you into one of the presses. For two days he was cursing you out up and down for disappearing without a word to anyone, but recently—and I swear it—he's been worried."

"Worried? Conklin?"

"Yeah," said Ross. "Every few hours he'd drop by my desk and say, 'I wonder where Revere could be. Stuie, do you think he's in trouble maybe? That's a bad neighborhood he lives in. Give him a ring, Stuie. See if he answers.' So I'd give you a ring, but you never answered."

"Figures," said George. "I wasn't there."

"Which brings me to the point, again, George. Where the hell have you been?"

"Stuie," George started, "if I told you right off the bat, you'd think I was nuts. I think we both can use five or six quick ones before it'll all start making sense. As a matter of fact, I'm not at all sure I believe it myself."

"It better be a real good one, or Conklin'll have your ass."

"Oh, it is, Stuie," said George. "It is."

They sat next to each other in front of a long mahogany bar in a small downstairs room east of the Plaza. The air had not yet taken on the eye-smarting smoky consistency it would have in several more hours; the small upright piano on the dais was still untended. The only sounds to be heard were the comforting background hubbub of conversation and the equally comforting rattle and tinkle of glasses, ice, and swizzle sticks. The atmosphere was exceptionally conducive to telling all. And, with the aid of his half-dozen quick ones, George told all.

Ross whistled, or tried to whistle. A certain stony lack of coordination was beginning to show. "Jee-zus," he said. "You mean that for a week you've been holed up with a gang of crooks in the Park who've been forging Plaid stamps?"

"Royal Purple stamps."

"'S unimportant." Stuie waved the consideration aside with a gesture that nearly upset his Scotch highball. "The point is, you've discovered a gang."

"Well, they actually discovered *me,* and besides,

they're not really a gang. They're sort of—well—a family, I guess."

"And one of these nuts has been getting away with stuff from the art museum, too?"

George began to feel slightly uncomfortable. "Well, yes and no, Stuie. I mean, he's—"

Ross stopped him abruptly with a raised hand whose palm hovered about an eighth of an inch from George's nose. Ross's eyes were shining.

"Kee-rist, what a scoop. What an everloving beautiful scoop! I can see it now, over our bylines: 'Central Park Syndicate Broken by *Alarum*.' 'Seize Art Treasures and Counterfeiting Plates Worth Fortune.' It'll be the biggest thing since V-E day!"

"No," said George.

"A second-coming head. I can see it. What do you mean, 'No'?" he added suspiciously.

"I mean no, Stuie. N-O, no. This one's not for print."

"What do you mean, not for print? Who are you, the President or somebody? Off the record? Thank you, Mr. Revere."

"Stuie, you're drunk. But listen to me. I'm involved in this one. Me. George Revere, your buddy. Does that mean anything? Who rolled you out of that hotel on Twenty-third Street at three A.M. and told Iris you had a dizzy spell in my apartment? Who has laid out the Gardens page so many times for you that he's beginning to look like a nasturtium? Who—"

"Enough, enough. I'll start to cry," said Ross. "You won't be involved, Georgie. You're an innocent accomplice."

"You mean an unwitting bystander."

"Yeah. That's what you are. You've got beans to worry about, so why are you worried?"

"I just don't want them in any trouble, Stuie. They've all been great to me, and I don't think I should make a big thing out of it, that's all."

Ross looked at him narrowly. "What's up between

you and the chick?" he said, pushing his face up close to George's.

"Well, that has nothing to do with it, Stuie. Hell, I mean it's just that—why should I bring the cops down on them? They never did anything to hurt me."

"So that's it. Score one for Stuie." Ross sat back, contented, and drained his glass. "Two more Peter Dawsons," he said to the bartender, and then turned back to George. "How do you know they didn't bop you in the first place?"

George was aghast. "Why, that's impossible. Absurd."

"Why?"

"They've been treating me like . . . well, like a member of their . . . group."

"So much the better. They know who you are—they've been stripping your apartment and hypnotizing you into signing checks or something."

"Checks against what? My thirty-five dollars in the _Alarum_ Credit Union?"

"Something else, then. They might be playing a smooth game."

"Stuie, you're out of your mind."

"You're the one that's been out of your mind for a good week, old man. Look, George, I like you. I think you've had a narrow escape playing around with these . . . these overgrown delinquents. You're lucky to be back to normal. Now, suppose you go home, get a good night's sleep, and tomorrow we'll explain the whole thing to Conklin and see if it'll make a story. With a good twenty column inches, he might not be nearly as mad."

"I can't just leave without saying something to them, Stuie. Be reasonable."

Ross took a deep breath and swiveled around to face George again. "She's not for you, kid. What the hell do you know about these people, anyway? They're bums, they're crooks, they're out-and-out criminals. Sure, they were nice to you—they probably saw you were a prize after they clobbered you, so they took you home, patched you up, and now they're working you into some kind of neat blackmail game. Come to think of it, I called your place about a week ago and some broad picked up the telephone. I thought it was a wrong number, but I'm not so sure now."

"Aw, Stuie, I don't think—"

"You're damn right, you don't think. You must have been hit even harder than you thought if you can't see what's been going on. Think about it."

George thought. Somehow, though, everything refused to come into focus. Bits and pieces of the past week floated through his mind like wisps of some cinematic jigsaw puzzle: the press clicking out stamps, Lynn's eyes staring into his that night at the Place, the clean light of dawn over The Lake, El Greco's strange collection, Freddy, Lynn, Lynn, Lynn . . .

"I can't go back with you, Stuie. Not right now, anyway."

"You're taking your life in your hands, George."

Shouldn't it always be that way? George thought. *Shouldn't my life always be in my own hands?* "Please, Stuie, hold off for a while. Let me go back there, knowing who I am, and see if it makes a difference. If they've been friends up to now, one more day won't hurt. They won't know I've recovered."

"You're playing with fire. Look, George. If you're going to do it, at least call me tomorrow so that I'll know everything's all right. I won't say anything to Conklin until I hear from you."

"Conklin will probably answer the phone; I don't want to get involved with him at this point."

"You're right. Look. Suppose I call you at your apartment around noon tomorrow. That way everything will be kosher."

"This is silly."

"It's idiotic," agreed Ross. "But it's nuts only because you're showing distinct signs of nuttiness yourself. Why the hell don't you just go back to your place and forget the whole thing?"

"I can't, Stu. Not now. There's something I've got to find out."

"About the chick?"

"No, about myself. Stu, play ball with me just for a little while. OK, I'll be at my place by noon tomorrow. I'll know by then."

"You've decided, George?"

"Yeah, Stuie. We have an outing scheduled for to-night, and I want to be there."

Ross got up stiffly. "An outing?" he asked.

"An outing," George said as they walked toward the door. "The Friends of Central Park, having cheerfully been guilty of trespassing, counterfeiting, and general mayhem, will tonight add hijacking to the list."

"Liquor?" asked Ross incredulously.

"Light," said George.

A black Buick hardtop convertible swerved into Trans-verse Road Number Two at Eighty-sixth Street and de-scended at a good rate of speed into the roadway that channeled through the Park. The hour was late and the traffic was light; the car sped on alone, its headlights carving a bright tunnel out of the heavy darkness.

Two massive figures sat hunched in the front seat. The driver seemed annoyed at his companion, who was nervously and lengthily expressing various misgivings to him.

"For Christ's sake, shut up, Herman," said the driver at last. "It ain't the first pile we've heisted, an' it won't be the last. What're you so worked up about?"

"It ain't the job, George," said Herman. "It's this creepy road. Why do we have to cut through the Park? It makes me nervous."

"We'll be out in two minutes," George Castello as-sured him. "Besides, we're down here on the highway. You couldn't even see the Park up there if you looked for it."

"I know," Herman said, still unconvinced, "but I just don't like this place. Step on it, will ya?"

Castello stepped on it.

Just as the car had turned into the Transverse, Freddy, watching closely from a nearby stone abutment, turned a powerful flashlight toward the tip of a flagpole that was barely visible above the trees in the distance. The beam lit up, for a minute, the golden figure of an eagle, standing angrily and precariously on its small golden ball far above a Park power station beside the road.

George, who had been watching the eagle carefully, saw the light and began a slow count, as Freddy had instructed him.

"One . . . Two . . ." he began and heard a whoosh as a car passed near the spot where he was lying, almost on the edge of the asphalt, at the junction of the main road and the power-station driveway. "Three . . . Four." On the count of four he jumped to his feet and quickly swung a barricade across the traffic lane. A blinking light began to illuminate the words "Detour" and "Police," as well as a black arrow pointing into the driveway. "Five . . . Six . . . Seven . . ."

At the count of ten the Buick's headlights knifed across the sign, and he drove back into the hedges.

"What the hell was that, George?" said Herman in alarm as his partner braked the auto and swung it into the driveway.

"That's funny," Castello said, "I don't remember there being a cutoff here," but he had little time to meditate on his suspicions; his headlights quickly lit up a tree standing in the center of the road, and he braked again, sending Herman thumping lightly against the windshield.

"That's funny," said Castello again. Obviously the evening was turning into a series of hilarities for him. "What's a tree doing in the middle of the street?"

"I don't like this place, George," whined Herman, rubbing his forehead. "It's jinxed, I told ya."

Castello threw the transmission into reverse and then stared with amazement at his rear-view mirror. His backup lights had illuminated another tree, which now blocked the way they had come. George Revere had swung the roadblock into the bushes as the car had passed and had just managed to roll this second potted tree into position. He now lay in the shadows, puffing like a harpooned grampus.

The nervousness in Herman's eyes had gone by this time, to be replaced by simple fear.

"Let's get out, George. I don't like this."

"I don't like it either. There's something very f—" Castello reached over and killed the engine, leaving his speculations on the situation hanging in midair. "C'mon," he said, "let's get out and see what's going on."

"We're not getting out of the car, are we?" Herman decided that he would not be nearly so terrified inside the car as outside.

"How can we get out if we don't get out?" asked Castello reasonably. "I'll leave the lights on."

He opened the door and stepped out onto the gravel. Herman hesitated for a moment before he followed. "I don't like it," he muttered just as reasonably.

They stood on opposite sides of the car, peering into the velvet darkness just beyond its lights. There was no sound other than the low, steady throbbing of a summer night in the Park, punctuated at intervals by Herman's nasal breathing. Gradually, however, both men became aware of another: the occasional drone of automobiles sweeping merrily along the road from which they had been so precipitously detoured.

"Geez, George," said Herman plaintively. "This whole thing gives me the creeps. I said not to cut through the Park, din' I? You know the place gives me the willies. Geez, look at it out there. It's black. I can't see a—"

"Shut up," said Castello. He was examining the potted tree which stood in back of the car, almost touching the bumper. He was working hard on a line of deductive thought, which kept eluding him. "This tree," he said.

Herman nodded. He wasn't sure what else he could do.

"This tree," Castello continued. "It wasn't here when we came."

"Sure it was, George," said Herman. "Remember, we nearly cracked up in it."

"That's the other tree, stupid. There. This one is behind us."

"Oh!" Something was puzzling Herman. "So how come we din' hit it?"

"What?"

"The tree."

"Which tree?"

The conversation was becoming too deeply involved with trees to suit Herman. Needless to say, he had never heard of the ones in the forest which cast no shadow, or the falling ones which nobody hears, or even the forest which nobody can see for them. All he could think of to say was, "The other tree. The one we din' hit."

"Somebody must have put it there."

"They shouldn't of done that, George. We coulda gotten hurt."

"Shut up. That tree," Castello said almost to himself as he grasped for the thought, "must have been put there while we were in the car."

"Which tree?" asked Herman, who was still trying to get the trees straight in his mind.

"Shut up," said Castello.

Herman was getting more and more uncomfortable. The darkness, the background noises, and the smothering oppressiveness of the empty night were reminding him painfully of that similar night the previous week when he had nearly sat down on that *thing* in the Park. He scuffled his feet nervously on the gravel; the sharp, crunching sound seemed to intensify his feeling of vulnerability to the hosts of evil spirits that exist in those dim never-never lands outside the bright neon glare of Broadway and Forty-second Street.

Just then Herman felt his eyes magnetically drawn to a deeper patch of shadow that had separated from the surrounding trees, and he saw the gorilla.

For the brief interval of time it took him to distinguish the gorilla from its eerie background, he stood rooted to the spot—unable to move, unable to speak. Slowly he felt pinpricks spread over his scalp, getting each hair follicle on fire, until the entire top of his head was alive in a network of electric tingling. Before his exopthalmic gaze, the figure became more distinct against the night.

Unfortunately, Herman was, at this point, in no position to look at the unusual sight of a gorilla roaming through Central Park with the cool detached interest such an event deserved. A connoisseur of gorillas, for instance, might have noticed the unmistakable points of similarity between this particular primate and Culver City Charlie, who has had screen credits stretching back to *Mighty Joe Young* and *King Kong*. Herman was no gorillaphile, however; all he could assimilate in the dimness beyond the headlights were a large quantity of hair and a pair of wicked incisors. Then he screamed.

"What the—" said Castello, whirling to see what had happened to his partner. By that time it was too late. If Herman had been wearing rubber-soled shoes, the effect would not have been unlike that of an Allard-Cadillac dragging on a gravel course: a screech, a shower of stones, the smell of burning rubber, and a faint breeze. In Herman's case, it was the smell of burning neoprene. Before Castello could finish his sentence, Herman had passed the first post and was holding the rail position in the stretch.

"—hell is going on here," Castello finished, coming around the side of the car. Then, as his eyes adjusted to the reduced light level, he also caught sight of the gorilla.

Feeling that it had not made its presence felt as forcibly on Castello as it had on his partner, the gorilla moved a few steps closer to the automobile, waving one arm in a vaguely threatening manner. It was a heavy arm, and Lynn, who was stifling inside the heavy suit, barely managed to wave it around convincingly. Nevertheless, Castello got the idea. He took a step backward and said, "Hey!"

Obviously pleased with this maneuver, he took another step backward and said, "Hey!" again. Then Lynn waved once more, and, as in a magic act, Castello disappeared. There was another shower of gravel.

The next three hundred seconds or so became a blur of movement centering on the empty automobile, which rested forlornly between the two large potted plants in the driveway. George Revere jumped up from his hiding place in the bushes; flicking off the car's lights, he lifted the hood and proceeded methodically to unscrew the battery holder. Meanwhile, Lynn, who had tottered back into the shadows of the surrounding trees, began to remove her hirsute costume, borrowed for the occasion from a surprisingly good selection of life-size outfits in the puppet house. Freddy had left his post at the entrance to the Transverse as soon as he had given his signal; he now stood in back of George.

This hum of activity was being generated while Sally, several hundred feet away, around a bend in the road, was closely watching the two dazed occupants of the car conversing animatedly; if they showed any signs of deciding to brave an immediate return, she was ready to signal Lynn, Freddy, and George to beat a strategic retreat.

It was not necessary. The whole operation lasted barely another two minutes. George lifted out the battery and handed it to Freddy. Freddy in turn handed him the dead battery from the Place, which had been secreted in the hedges alongside the driveway. George clamped the old unit into place and slammed down the hood. Then he and Lynn, who had shed the last pieces of her unflattering disguise, quickly replaced the potted trees to their normal positions at the door of the power station, and Freddy disappeared with the loot—all thoroughly rehearsed cogs in a well-oiled mechanism.

"Let there be light," George murmured, scooping up the gorilla costume, and with Lynn, double-timing up a narrow flight of steps carved in the rocks leading to the Park level.

"Something fishy is going on around here," Herman was saying brightly, but there was nobody to hear: Castello was intent on the problem of deciding his next step (a procedure that had to minimize the part of the police, or any other form of free publicity); and Sally had left the vicinity a few moments before, at a low signal from Freddy.

Silence descended on the scene.

George and Lynn dodged through the trees and bushes, tripping over rocks and roots, exchanging gasps of laughter as they ran.

"Did you see . . . ?"

"Did you hear . . . ?"

"When he . . ."

"When I . . ."

Abruptly George staggered to a stop, and clutching a tree, lapsed into a long, helpless paroxysm of laughter that continued until he fell onto the heap of gorilla skin that had dropped to his feet. Trying unsuccessfully to catch her breath, Lynn joined him; the two lay together, laughing uncontrollably in the warmth of the summer night and their own happiness.

Slowly their breathing became more and more regular, and George's arms found their way around Lynn's waist. They faced each other and kissed: a lingering kiss that fused them into one body of feeling, one body of thought.

When they separated, George could see the dim outline of her head against his shoulder.

"George," she said, "whoever you really are, I would never want you to leave me. It could never be that important, could it?"

"Could what?" said George.

Lynn sat upright. "I mean, it would be the same for us no matter who we were—if you were a street cleaner and I were just another nine-to-five secretary."

"I couldn't see you typing your life away. You're more the coffee-break sort."

"Oh, be serious, George. Just love me."

George had a strange feeling: more than any other time with Lynn, he was aware that he was speaking words to her—conscious, well-thought-out words in sentences, with subjects, predicates, objects, modifiers, clauses, and, occasionally, participles. It was an odd experience. He wondered if Lynn felt it also.

"I do love you, my darling. Whoever I am, I could never imagine not—"

He was about to finish with "loving you," but as he was trying to untangle the double negative, she came close to him once more; the thought was lost in the warm softness of their fur blanket. For one curious moment, as they sank into its folds, his eyes met the glassy stare of the gorilla, peering sightlessly at the gross invasion of his privacy. Then, in an instant, it was over, and George lost himself completely in Lynn.

Herman Krugwerksch and George Castello sat in the front seat of the Buick trying vainly to sort out reality from illusion. Everything seemed the same, but neither of them could forget the sinister implications of the trees in the road or the monster in the shadows that had routed them barely fifteen minutes before. Castello shrugged and put his foot on the gas pedal.

"I still got that spooky feeling, George," said Herman. "Something's gonna happen—I know something's gonna happen," he repeated as Castello turned the key in the ignition.

He was wrong, of course. Nothing happened.

9 How Mr. Cuttleworth Winked and George Thought He Understood

Promptly at 11:30 the next morning, George added another armload of Royal Purples to the growing stockpile at the Place and left for a stroll around the Park. He had a strange thrill of excitement and, in his pocket, the key to his apartment. The Buick's battery had been placed in the Place's lighting system; after a night of being charged with the city's current, it was providing light for Sally and Lynn to continue work on their gypsy routines, or, as Sally referred to them, the "crystal-ball one-acts." Freddy was surreptitiously engaged in hoeing a new plot just inside the Fifth Avenue wall at Ninety-third Street, which he believed would be perfect for eggplant.

It was a bright day of September; the sun blazed directly overhead, minimizing the size of shadows in which the few people populating the Park at that hour could find relief from the heat. George walked briskly across the bridle path, up the walk to Central Park West, and across to Eighty-seventh Street. Oddly enough, this, his first homecoming in almost ten days, produced no exotic sensations in him other than this slight excitement which was due, almost entirely, to a guilty feeling he had developed about his convert resumption of the second half of his double life. No chill of anticipation plucked at his spine, no gnawing presentiments dampened his palms. He felt a bit sheepish about the whole thing.

Yet, as he let himself into his apartment, he was momentarily startled. Although he thought his transition from the amnesiac had taken place with no traumas or blank spots, he certainly did not remember having left his apartment in such a shipshape condition. He closed the door behind him and looked around again. Had he really ever been this neat?

Stuie's words came back to him: perhaps they had known his identity. Was it at all possible? Could they have had access to his apartment for the past week?

He started to check randomly through his closets and his desk. Nothing appeared to be missing. True, he couldn't find his address book offhand, but his valuables—jewelry, television, checkbook, clothes, cash, typewriter, hi-fi—each of the few things he owned which had a trade-in value of over fifty dollars seemed to be in the right place. George sat down in the kitchen, puzzling over the phenomenon. Unless he did indeed have a blind spot (which was not completely unreasonable, he assured himself), somebody had been through his rooms since he had last been there.

But who?

He could think of no one else who had a key, unless Valerie had had a copy made before he repossessed her duplicate during one argument. George could not picture Valerie taking any opportunity to clean his apartment, but Stuie might have put her up to it. He would call Valerie and see.

Stymied momentarily by the loss of his address book, he got her number from Information and was about to dial when the phone rang. *Stuie*, he thought—*I suppose I can really ask him.* George didn't feel particularly like talking to Valerie, anyway; their last weekend hadn't been entirely amicable. He crumpled the scrap of notepaper with her number and tossed it into his wastebasket, where it dropped, unseen, on another small crumpled note lying at the bottom. Then he picked up the receiver.

"Yes, Stuie. No, everything's fine. I'm not sure, because I think someone might have been in my place. No. No, nothing missing. I can't imagine. I thought you might have some idea . . . Val, maybe? No, I didn't think so. Well, maybe. I'm still not clear about that night. I'm probably imagining things."

"Maybe you are and maybe you aren't," said Ross. "Are you back for good?"

"I'm really not sure, Stuie. I'd like to play this thing out to the end of the week, anyway. How's Conklin taking it?"

"Another few days won't make that much difference to his ulcers, I suppose, but I still think you're nutty as a fruitcake. If I were you, I'd get back in harness, write up the whole business, and settle back with a raise and, maybe, a promotion to the Desk."

"But you're not me. There are a few things I still have to figure out, but in any case I'll be back before next week is out. Honest."

"You don't have to play cross-my-heart with me, kiddo. Look, just tell me one thing. Is this broad worth it?"

"Christ, Stuie, I don't know. If I knew, I could settle this whole thing right now. I don't want to keep this Park thing up—it's getting sillier and sillier, now that I think of it. But on the other hand, I can't chuck her without a word. Believe me, Stuie, it isn't an easy thing to think about."

"That's the trouble with you bachelors," Ross said. "You take this whole damn thing too seriously. As long as it doesn't cost you money, it means you're in love, and you never know when to let go. Play the merry-go-round way, George. Every ride is different, and you can always try for the brass ring. But no ride is going to last forever. I bet I can get Alice, the new receptionist, for you on ten minutes' notice. She'd be crazy for a critic."

"Yeah, I know, Stuie. But I'll play this one my own way."

"Should I call you tomorrow?"

"Goddamn it, Stuie, you sound like my mother."

"That's me—Mother Ross. Nevertheless, I want to make sure everything's going according to Hoyle. Because if you hadn't answered me today, George boy, every blasted cop in the precinct would have been squatting in the Park until we knew why."

"OK, you're on. Tomorrow, same time, same station."

"Look, George. Don't do anything silly."

"No, Stuie, I won't. That's a promise. So long." *That's a promise*, he repeated to himself as he replaced the phone in its cradle.

He stood up in front of his desk and looked around the room. *What the hell am I doing?* was the thought recurring to him at more frequent intervals now. *If I leave my home today and go back to the Park, what makes me so sure I won't do the same tomorrow? And next week?*

Shaking his head as if to clear it, George walked back to the living room and sank down into the comfortably upholstered armchair in which he was accustomed to spend all periods of decision, indecision, and boredom. Was Lynn really worth it? came the question, and just as insistently it was answered, in the time-honored aggravating manner, with another question: Worth what? George knew quite clearly that he was not going to live in Central Park for the rest of his life; he also realized quite clearly that his residence there could probably be measured in terms of days now. Why should he give up a reasonable way of life—not an affluent life, mind, but a *reasonable* one—to embark on a picaresque wisp of an idea? Absurd. George snorted. This was the twentieth century; while astronauts were racing to the moon to get the first chance at magazine-serialization rights and endorsements, could he, George Revere, sink into a vagabond existence in the midst of a city of eight million people? Ridiculous.

But the question remained—where did Lynn fit in? Why, of course, in the act of bringing her into his life. Somehow, Sally, Freddy, and the Place under Belvedere Tower never entered into this picture of Lynn in his plans; Lynn would be a presence in his address book

like Val, or like what's-her-name in Conklin's office.
But the Park life was out.

Or was it? Could he really continue to have Lynn
now and then, shuttling back and forth indefinitely between the comparative reality of West Eighty-seventh
Street and the James M. Barrie world of Central Park?
There seemed to be no clear-cut answer. George was
not even sure he could think of a clear-cut question.

Could he continue to maintain his not unpleasant re-
lationship with Lynn while becoming, once again and
fulltime, George Revere? Of course. Why not?

Then what the hell was the problem?

Unfortunately, George was in this quandary simply
because he was swamped in his own subjectivity—he
was able to see no further than the next date to share a
two-on-the-aisle, with perhaps a drink at his place later.
His blind spot, whose presence he faintly realized but
whose nature continued to puzzle him, was simply this:
Lynn Harmony, being a sentient human being, had
something to say about any arrangement of which she
was to be a part.

Simple? Of course. Yet George, with a positive genius for taking things as they came and constructing a
dull universe circling about his not particularly impressive person, could not appreciate the fact that people—
especially women—were not put into this world for the
express purpose of submitting their behavior patterns to
his planning efforts. And so now he was slumped in an
armchair attempting to solve a problem that he was not
even sure existed. It was getting him nowhere. He finally arose, took one last look around the apartment,
and let himself out into the hall.

George thought of the many previous times when he
had simply walked out of his apartment: to go to the
office, to throw out the garbage, to pick up a Sunday
Times, to see a show. This time he felt no different; he
knew he would be back. Once before when he had left,
it had taken him a long while to return, but this time
things would be more routine. Still, the problem of the

clean apartment kept nagging him; he was beginning to think about Stuie's remarks again. Perhaps Stuie had been right; perhaps he had not called the wrong number that day.

"Glad to have you back, Mr. Revere. I hope you're feeling better."

George paused on the steps leading up to the sidewalk and saw the superintendent gazing down at him kindly from the row of garbage cans at the railing. "Hello, Mr. Cuttleworth," he said, brightening. "You're just the man I've been looking for."

"Glad to help out, if I can," said Mr. Cuttleworth, winking broadly and hitching his belt buckle with one hand.

"Would you know, by any chance, if I might have had a visitor while I was . . . er . . . during the past week while I was out of town?"

Mr. Cuttleworth's wink threatened to cost him the sight of one eye permanently. To George's relief, however, he finally reopened it; his smile was as broad as his drawl.

"I guess it's all right for my folks to have their lady friends up, Mr. Revere, as long as they behave themselves. If you know what I mean. We're pretty lib'ril here at the Cuttleworth Arms."

"Yes, I know, Mrs. Cuttleworth. But was anyone here while I was gone?"

"Was anything missing, Mr. Revere? You've got to watch them like a hawk, I always say. I would've liked to watch this one, though—especially while she was taking a bath."

"A bath?"

Mr. Cuttleworth shifted his weight off the garbage can and stepped down to George's level. "You can pick 'em, Mr. Revere—I've always said so. The missus and I, we're—"

"Mr. Cuttleworth, can you describe the girl who was here?"

"Describe her?"

"Yes. What did she look like? Can you remember?"
"I guess I can," said Mr. Cuttleworth.

Lynn stood in the doorway of an old apartment house
and watched the two men conversing across the street.
She had been strolling down Central Park West when
an almost irresistible urge to reconnoiter George's
apartment had overtaken her. She had turned into West
Eighty-seventh Street just in time to see George coming
up the front steps to talk to the super. She dodged into
the doorway and pressed herself against the far wall,
trying to straighten out her own whirling thoughts.

From where she stood she could see the old man de-
scribing someone to George—and Lynn knew who that
someone probably was. She felt a momentary pang of
sorrow at having given way to an irrational impulse for
housecleaning, a pang which was quickly eradicated by
a flash of anger and resentment at George for keeping
his obviously recovered identity a secret.

She peered out again. The old man was laughing
heartily at something he had just said. George looked
slightly puzzled and was nodding continuously. Lynn
watched them for a few moments, her eyes flashing. A
pickup truck sped down the street, momentarily crossing her field of view; she seized the opportunity to slip
out of the doorway and joined a ragged knot of people
who were ambling slowly toward the Park. As they
reached the corner she stole a quick glance backward;
George was still nodding, as if hypnotized, and she
could almost visualize the old superintendent winking.

She walked as if she were threading in and out of a
maze of furniture on her way through a dark room.
Each footstep deliberately followed the next with mechanical regularity, propelled forward by a slow and
monotonous timing mechanism. The pavement passed
under her tennis shoes like a Mack Sennett revolving
scenery drum; curbstones came and went—concrete, asphalt, dirt, and grass followed each other in unnoticed
sequence. At one point a car shrieked protestingly and

skidded to a stop a foot from her; Lynn did not even look up as the driver, fumbling with the window, penetratingly hurled after her some kindly suggestions as to her probable parentage and occupation.

The post-lunch crowd was filling the Park. Battalions of children descended again into their huge playground, slightly more subdued following their noon ration of strained applesauce and Metrecal; some slept. In addition, the *avant-grade* of the teen-age contingent were filtering in—a few diehard delinquents who spent their leisure time feeling the statuary or spelling out on the walls of the pedestrain tunnels some of the harder words they had learned. Surrounding them all, the old people, like an eternal breakwater against the tides of the generations, sat everlastingly on the rim of benches that lined each walk and path.

Lynn walked blindly through the crowds—bumping, brushing, shouldering, elbowing. Gradually the noises of traffic and shouting died away as she passed into the interior of the Park and began the slow ascent to the Belvedere Tower. Whatever thoughts she was turning over in her mind occupied her full attention; her face was expressionless, her progress trancelike. The grass under her feet gave way to stone as she began to climb the majestic flight of stairs leading up to the base of the Tower. A few scattered couples were milling around aimlessly on the terrace; the only sound was the click of a camera shutter as someone continuously experimented with different lighting and new angles.

Lynn moved unthinkingly to the edge of the parapet, where she bumped gently into a wooden-rail barrier, like a ship nudging its slip, and stopped. She stood against the fence; her eyes, still flashing, stared vaguely out over the broad landscape of water and meadows below. It was there, some thirty minutes later, that George found her.

It was not the consideration of legal punishment alone that prevented George from wreaking bodily havoc on

Lynn, although his thoughts had been running along that lurid line since he had left the ptotic Mr. Cuttleworth. Underneath his exterior vexation at Lynn for mysteriously having withheld his identity while making use of his apartment, there ran a strong current of warm, not solely humanitarian feeling toward her. At the moment, however, this current had collided head on with the ice water of the Suspicion Stream, and the resulting fog had somewhat clouded George's perception.

As he mounted to the terrace, all he could see in front of him was a semi-fiend in rather attractive human form who had kept him in amnesiac servitude for some nefarious purposes of her own, or her cohorts', and who had invaded the privacy of his three-room castle for God-knows-what Machiavellian reasons. Like Medusa, her hair writhed with a thousand snakes—but this may have been due to that fog which rose rapidly in front of his vision.

He walked to the railing and stood beside Lynn. Desperately he tried to phrase the first venom-filled question that would impart to this Jezebel the full horror, shock, and fury of his revelation. *Why didn't you tell me who I was?*, he thought. *What were you doing in my apartment?* No, too Victorian. *What have you done in my apartment?* Ambiguous. *Why didn't you tell me you knew?*

"Why didn't you tell me you knew?" asked Lynn in a sharp voice, still facing out over the parapet. "Why didn't you tell me?"

If someone had suddenly removed the stone terrace from below George's feet, leaving him suspended in midair while his stomach plummeted down to the foot of the cliff, he couldn't have been more taken aback. Somehow, he had never considered his own actions as being up for review; this was due, no doubt, to that certain blind spot we have noticed before in his thought processes. The idea that there was something wrong in his carefully reasoned plan to withhold his identity from this girl while he decided if he would maintain their re-lationship—this idea struck him as being nobody's business but his own.

At this moment he was transfixed by an obvious difference of opinion between Lynn and himself on this interesting point.

"Why didn't you tell me you knew?" Lynn repeated in a flat voice without turning around.

"What for?" said George. "It wouldn't have been any great news to you."

Lynn looked out over the blistered landscape for a long time. "I was afraid to tell you, and I was right," she said. "I hoped you would want to share your precious Revere with me, but I didn't want to find out."

George was silent. He still could not quite understand how the initiative had been wrested from him so easily. He had the feeling of a tennis player who has gone from match-point to advantage-out in two volleys.

"That all sounds very fine," he said harshly, "but it has nothing to do with the fact that you probably knew all about me from the beginning. It suited you to have an isolated playmate hanging around like a Saint Bernard."

Lynn wheeled around angrily. "And what were you planning for me in your future? Why did you come back at all? For a Saint Bernardine?"

Once more George looked deeply into her blue eyes, but this time there was an unaccustomed shield of high-tension electricity holding him at distance.

"I suppose the fact that you've been living in my apartment while I was suffering the tortures of the damned trying to figure out who I was— I suppose you think that was OK?" he said.

"I haven't been living in your apartment," said Lynn. "Mr. Cuttleworth saw you!"

"Good for Mr. Cuttleworth. Did he also see you sneaking out to the Park every now and then for a romp with your new toy?"

George snorted. "Now, what the hell is that supposed to mean?"

"Any damn thing you want it to," said Lynn. "Why don't you just go away? Go back to your two-bit newspaper and leave the living to us."

"If that's the way you want it," said George.

"That's the way I want it."

"Fine," said George. He felt anger welling up inside his throat like a damned river. His voice was strident, cracked. "I don't know what your angle has been, but I'm finished with the whole lunatic bunch of you."

Lynn's only answer was to start turning slowly away, back to the vista below the Tower. George's voice rose as he felt her slipping away from him.

"And you and your mother can go on doing whatever the hell it is you do. I've got to get back to my two-bit apartment, which you seem to like so much, and count all my silverware again."

Before the words were completely out—before he had a chance to realize what he had allowed himself to say—Lynn had whirled around, one open palm extended, and had struck him a stinging blow on the side of his face. George's felt a rush of resentment; Lynn stood glaring at him, her face registering her wrath and embarrassment at George's remark and at her reaction. They remained staring at each other for several long, unclocked moments. The wave that had abruptly broken, showering down its accumulated burden of fright and uncertainty, was now ebbing from George's consciousness: a slow draining that left him at once bewildered and helpless. He knew he had gone too far, but in an unknown deeper sense, he was aware that he had not gone nearly far enough.

He could not bring himself to meet the anguish in Lynn's eyes. As he shifted his gaze desperately, in order to cover up the momentary paralytic void that had taken over his body, he slowly began to realize that several people were looking at him curiously; the man with the camera appeared to be about to snap his picture. George suddenly felt the absurdity of his position.

Lynn turned her back once more and resumed her

sightless stare at the Manhattan horizon, over the tops of miles of Park trees stretching out before her—a deep-pile carpet of bright green. Without attempting another word, George spun on his heel and walked quickly away. He did not look back. Not that it would have mattered if he had—he would have had to climb over the parapet, lower himself onto the rough-cut rock face of the cliff, and inch his way carefully over the rocks, without daring to think about the seventy-five-foot drop to the water below, before he could have noticed that Lynn was crying.

"We're all interdependent, Stuie. That's our trouble. Too damn' independent."

"You don't mean independent, George. You said underdependent."

"Yeah, that's what I meant. Women are too damn' undependable."

George and Stuie Ross sat across from each other in an uncomfortable, plastic-upholstered booth that faced the same bar at which they had talked the previous night. The small cellar again had that afternoon look of tentative doom; it was almost inconceivable that in a few hours every stool and chair would be filled and the upright piano on the dais would be segueing from "It's All Right with Me" to "Little Girl Blue."

After leaving the Tower, George had walked straight to the nearest telephone booth in order to call Ross. His message was brief and to the point: "I'm going to get drunk at Hugo's. Join me when you can." Ross had joined him within the hour and had caught up with very little trouble.

The table in front of them carried traces of their last six rounds—a few glasses, some odds and ends of potato chips, and an untidy mound of coasters, napkins, and swizzle sticks on a field of wet rings. Ross slumped back in the booth, carefully stirring his Scotch with exaggerated precision. Every once in a while he would chuckle to himself over some secret joke between his drink and himself. George sat hunched over the table, his elbows set wide apart and his chin resting on his hands. He stared at Ross accusingly.

"You don't understand a word I'm talking about."

Ross chuckled. "Oh, yes, I do. You're saying that we're all my brother's keeper."

"You don't have a brother," said George.

"Well, if I did, we would be his keeper."

"What the hell kind of a brother would need a keeper? Is your whole family insane?"

Ross's expression changed in a flash; the amber glow of alcoholic sunshine faded into 86.8-proof sullenness.

"My brother and his family have nothing to do with this. Anyone who insults my brother is a cad."

George waved the whole affair away with an expansive gesture, striking his knuckles painfully on the edge of the booth.

"You're my frien', Stuie. I love your brother like my brother."

"Tha's better," said Ross.

There was another silence, punctuated by Ross's erratic chuckles.

"You see," said George, "we're all brothers, in a way."

"You know," said Ross, "you're right."

"We're all brothers. We all have to hang."

Ross was startled. "Whadaya mean, hang? Why hang?"

"I dunno," replied George, puzzled. "I think Franklin said it. We all gotta hang or else we'll get hanged."

"Franklin who?"

"Franklin, Benjamin. Tha's who."

"Oh." The implication that he was headed for the gallows seemed to upset Ross unduly. "I still don't see why they have to hang us. We haven't done anything."

"We do things all the time," said George. "Tha's the whole point. We're always doing things that affect other people."

"You're right, Georgie. We ought to hang for that."

"Every time I breathe," continued George, enlarging on his theme, "I affect everyone in New York."

Ross whistled. "You oughta try brushing your teeth more often," he said.

George ignored him and went on. "I affect an Arab somewhere in Libya."

"Wow," exclaimed Ross, in awe of his friend's powers.

"You bet," said George.

They both considered this proposition in silence for a while. George started to shake his head slightly from side to side in some interior negation; the shaking became progressively more violent, until his neck seemed in danger of twisting off.

"No," he cried, causing the bartender and two waiters to turn around in surprise. "No! If I wanted to live in the Park, I'd be a—a squirrel."

"Why would you want to live in the Park?" asked Ross.

"I wouldn't," said George. "The whole idea is abs— absilly. I would be out of my mind to live in the Park with gypsy gardeners."

Ross did not quite grasp the concept of Romany tillers of the soil. However, he had found something to amuse himself in a renewed glass of Scotch, and George went on patiently.

"Look, I have it all figured out. I'm a good guy, like you meet every day, right?" He didn't wait for a reply, which was just as well. "I'm OK. Everything about me is OK. But some people are destined to live in apartments on Eighty-seventy Street; others are destinated the same to live in Central Park. They're two different kinds of people. She's from one side of Central Park West and I'm from the other. What can you expect? Why should I live in a cave when I've got a desk? After a hard day's work listening to Conklin, I can't come home to a tree, can I? I mean, I could get arrested, for God's sake! What has she got that I haven't?"

George sat back in the booth, satisfied. He had

poured out everything that had been stuffed into odd corners of his mind, and this speech had settled the whole affair to his satisfaction. "Nothing," was his triumphant answer. "No."

"Bravo," cheered Ross. "There're lotsa good broads in the sea." He brought his wristwatch slowly into focus. "My God," he whispered reverently, "it's almost seven. Let's get outa here before Iris kills me."

He motioned for the bill, and they made their wavering way to the street. A trail of bluish cigarette smoke spiked with samples of other distilled vapors followed them into the flat brightness of the cooling evening. The pavement, scorched unmercifully during the day, thankfully exhaled the heat from a million pores.

They wove up Fifth Avenue, finally—past the glassy glitter of the newer buildings which have elbowed their way into the masonry, marble, and brass escutcheons of the nineteen-twenties. As they moved into the hotel belt, with the broad expanse of the Plaza on their left and General Sherman eternally, if a bit greenishly, following Victory dead ahead, George pulled a wad of crumpled paper out of his pocket. He looked at it closely and then held his hand out to Ross.

"Stamps, Stuie. Royal Purple trading stamps. Best buy by far. Whadaya think of that?"

Ross didn't think anything of it.

"Turning 'em out like hotcakes," George said. He stopped in front of a large wastebasket that contained the day's offering from people who did not wish to make New York dirty—two beer cans, a New York *Alarum,* an umbrella, and half of a watermelon. On top of these gifts to the Sanitation Department George began adding a shredded layer of the small purple oblongs. "Ashes to ashes and garbage to garbage," he intoned. Somewhere, underfoot, a subway rumbled through.

"Tha's a lotta stamps," said Ross. "What happens when they get back to the company?"

"Probably nothing," said George. "The more stamps

the better. Barrels and barrels of stamps. They'll say it was all because of their wonnerful advertising job."

He finished tipping his handful of stamps into the can and then looked up for a brief moment at the Park. The sun, low on the horizon and hidden beyond the jutting buildings, threw long, dim shadows against the green warmth of the Park. The massed trees stood in front of them, a crater of life in the midst of the stone augularities of the surrounding cliffs. As they watched, the green began clouding into blue. In front of them a horse pulled impatiently on his hansom cab and neighed quietly.

"The hell with it," said George. "I don't want to go near it. Let's cut across through here."

He turned on his heel, and they walked carefully down Fifty-eighth Street, into the deepening dusk.

10 *How Sol Berman Educed a Paradox*

"I bet this is the best showing by any coupon since Schulte's quit," said Sol Berman proudly to his staff. "You boys have done a wonderful advertising job."

His staff shuffled its feet nervously.

"Maybe we don't always see together eye to eye," continued Berman, "but these results ain't lying—you done a good day's work. If we're gonna be honest, though, you can't say I didn't help out a little, right?"

"No, sir," the staff said.

"A slogan here, a critical there; it all adds up now and then. A college education is good for a young man, that's why I hired you. But it ain't everything—it ain't experience; that's why it's me doing the hiring, not you."

"Yes, sir," said the staff.

"OK," said Berman. "As long as we all can understand the same language. Now, let's look at this week's pictures."

The "pictures" to which Berman referred were an important output of the marketing staff, which had taken many pains and efforts to make them as pretty and as intelligible for Berman as possible. Their official title was *A Weekly Summary of Distribution, Redemption, and Sales of Royal Purple Trading Stamps: Trend Analysis, Marketing, and Forecasting.* Since Berman thought this title was an excessively long-winded one to describe the myriads of multicolored graphs that were presented to him every week at his Monday-morning conference, he chose to call them, simply and directly, "the pictures." It was an unknowing tribute to the frustrated modern artists who worked nights for a charting company turning out these and similar presentations for Berman's Bazaar.

It was the third weekly conference since Berman last appeared in these pages; the increasing scope of good news had made him begin to look forward to them. For in the short span of twenty-one days following the technical completion of his staff's "good job"—more formally referred to as the *Annual Motivational Research and Marketing Plans*: *Phase One Instrumentation*—the thin red lines on all his charts had shown a most encouraging determination to ascend steeper slopes than ever before. Needless to say, Berman was elated. His staff was elated. Even his Marketing Director's mother was elated.

"It looks like the printing boys can't turn out enough coupons now, eh? Nice, nice."

This last referred, simultaneously, to the prospect of increased sales, to Berman's growing paternalistic affection for his successful marketing staff and to the pretty pictures. He was looking specifically at a chart entitled *Circulations,* which indicated the quantities of Royal Purples that had been placed in the hands of presumably eager dealers all over the city. For the edification of the more scientifically minded reader, as well as the occasional advertising man who may be skimming this story while waiting for the home finance manager of the Chase Manhattan Bank to approve his loan, the important segment of this chart is hereby reproduced in full:

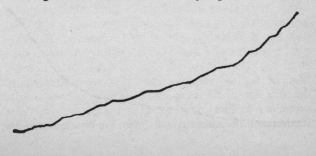

It was indeed, as Berman expressed it, nice, nice.

"As you see," the Marketing Director was saying, "the upward trend is continuing, showing a net increase of some two million stamps over the index one month ago. This represents an increased print order of some four hundred and fifty thousand stamps over the four-week period, or an average of—ah—one hundred twelve thousand, five hundred stamps per week." The Director (whose name, which should be recorded for posterity, was Leslie Onandorfer) had carefully reviewed these figures the night before with his mother (whose name was Mrs. Sturdley; she had shed Leslie's name along with Mr. Onandorfer some years before) and had even impressed her with their portents of miraculous events to come.

Sol Berman gazed with rapture at the incipient Everest on the easel before him. "Two million this month, imagine. It's like they were stuffing pillows with them."

Leslie overlooked this irreverence with his characteristic understanding of Berman's thought processes and his natural talent for survival. He replied by setting up another similar chart on the easel, thus allowing Berman to contemplate a still prettier picture. This one was labeled *Redemptions*, and its message, conveyed in neatly dashed lines like red snowshoe marks, could have been a scoreboard for a successful Baptist preacher. Leslie let the good word sink in.

"As you see," he repeated, "the effect of the Phase One campaign has been reflected, to a greater degree, in redemptions. Increased awareness of the superior marketability of Royal Purples had caused redemptions to jump three million, five hundred thousand stamps over the past one-month period, for a gain of almost ten percentage points a week. This is a total redemption rate, I might point out, of almost triple our moving average over the previous fiscal year."

"You bet," said Sol Berman, impressed.

"The especially gratifying part," Leslie went on proudly, "is the reduction in lag time between circulations and redemptions, which means that there is developing a geometric multiplication advantage factor between our wholesale deliveries and our customer point-of-sales acceptance."

"Sure," said Berman. He appeared to be somewhat less than sure. "You guys all listen to Onondaga there." Berman had a brother in upstate New York, which may explain his offhand butchery of Leslie's name.

Leslie, who considered this lapse one of Berman's most boorish traits, lightly brushed aside his irritation and stepped back into the warm precincts of the staff. It was the turn of the Director of Sales to pick up where he had left off.

The Director of Sales was Berman's wife's cousin, a burly fast-talking man who had started in business some twenty years before on the Lower East Side of New York selling rolls of toilet paper with Adolf Hitler's face printed on every square. His double-breasted pinstripe suit, slightly pinched at the waist, stood out against the forest of gray J. Press that surrounded him, making him resemble the Ugly Duckling in the bosom of its unappreciative family.

"Christ, Sol," he began, "I ain't got none of these ———— lines to go up and down. Money, we're makin'. On that you can quote me. The stuff's turning over like crazy, and with that shipment of seconds we scrounged from the toaster outfit, we oughta be able to raise the ante this month to about twenny-five per, without commissions and kickback."

The gray phalanx winced in unison. Berman, who should have been listening to this narration with shining eyes while visions of dollar signs danced in his head, merely sat back and looked abstractedly at the ceiling. It was a comparatively dull ceiling, as ceilings go—a stamped tin sheet showing five or six different layers of paint through successive levels of flaking.

"The coupons are moving like ———— chopsticks in China. For the past month, we've been pushin' them inta stores with rakes, they've béen so hot for our bodies."

Berman nodded once or twice. "Go on, Morris."

"That's it," Morris said. "If you want the ———— red lines should run around a chart, I'll have one of the boys whip one up. But from me you can take it, it's been a good month. And, by the way, Sol, here's something I found in the elevator room the other day."

He winked broadly and dumped a sheaf of grease-stained paper booklets on Berman's desk. "From me to you, Sol—a complete set of *Smilin' Jack in the Land of the Amazons* and one extra copy of *Superman and Superwoman* like you've been asking me for for the past year."

"Thanks, Morris," said Berman. It was obvious that he was distracted. A vagrant thought, blown into his head by Leslie, was incubating slowly. Berman was working on the quiet puzzle without success. Finally he turned to the staff.

"Look, Onondaga. You said we've gotten rid of a couple million Purples last month, right?"

Leslie took a cautious breath. "Yes, sir," he said, not taking any chances.

"OK. So we pushed a couple million. So how come three and a half were redeemed. I mean, how can we cash in more coupons than we make? It ain't ever happened before."

Leslie was relieved. "That's right, Mr. Berman, it

ain't—uh—hasn't. That's what I meant when I said that
the lag between redemptions and circulations was being
reduced. You see, sir, with the increased emphasis on
the vitality of Royal Purples, people who might not normally want to redeem their cou—stamps right away are
rushing down to take advantage of the bargains. They
can't wait."

"Hoarders," said Berman.

"You could say that," said Leslie.

"I did," said Berman.

"Anyway, that's the principle. Last month our redemption rate surpassed our circulation rate for the first
time."

"It ain't ever happened before, and I don't like it,"
said Berman.

Leslie could not quite grasp the problem. It was all
crystal clear to him. Like normal distributions and
three-sigma limits. "There's really nothing not to like,
Mr. Berman," he said, choking slightly over the double
negative.

"Shut up for a minute, Onondaga, and let me think."
Berman thought. He absently picked up one of the
books Morris had left on his desk and began riffling
through it.

"Let's try this one against the flagpole," he finally
said. "This red business over here is all the coupons we
make, right?"

"That's right, sir," said Leslie. "That chart is a cumulative total of all our circulations."

"Fine," said Berman. "And that one with the
dashes—that's the total we've cashed in from the beginning?"

"Yes, sir," said Leslie. "This chart is our cumulative
redemptions."

"Hmmmm." Berman put down *Smilin' Jack* and
stared at the two offending charts. "I don't like it," he
said. Suddenly he snapped his fingers. "I got it. Put one
of them on top of the other!"

Morris obediently placed one cardboard chart in front of the other on the easel.

"Shmuck!" screamed Berman. "I mean I want to see the two lines on the same chart. Run!"

Everyone ran. Leslie picked up the two graphs and fled, accompanied by his gray assistants. Berman picked up his comic book again and riffled through it, emitting an occasional low whistle and drumming his fingers impatiently on his blotter.

"Jeez, Morris," he said finally, "I don't see how they can allow stuff like this on the market."

"They don't," said Morris.

Just then Leslie rushed in with a revised chart, on which two associates and an assistant had worked feverishly. Berman surveyed the results, which looked something like this:

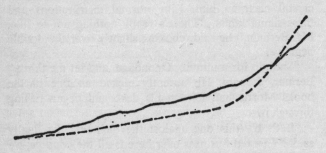

"Aha," exclaimed Berman. "Now, Onondaga— Columbia boy—come here a minute."

"Princeton," said Leslie weakly.

"So let it be Princeton. Would you kindly explain to me again how come we are cashing in more coupons than we are making."

Leslie stared at the chart for a moment. It was all crystal clear. "That isn't what it means, Mr. Berman," he started. "You see, there is always a lag between redemptions and circulations. I mean, the other way around." He laughed nervously. "It takes a while for people to turn in their trading stamps after they receive them, and it takes another—er—while between the time we make them and get them."

"So far I understand. You understand, Morris?"

"So far," said Morris.

"Go on," said Berman.

Leslie laughed nervously. "So, of course, we always have this lag, as you can see on this chart."

"Get to last month."

"Last month," Leslie continued, "you see that both our rate of circulations and our rate of redemptions have increased sharply, showing the immediate effect of our advertising campaign on the wholesalers, as well as its—uh—multiplication, or rather geometric—er— leverage when transmitted to the ultimate customer. You see, we have here a case in which the *redemptions*—no, the *circulations*, have actually been surpassed by the cumulative—er—total . . ."

Leslie Onandorfer trailed off in silence. That night he would tell his mother that it was the most curious feeling he had had since his father once pulled a chair out from under him. His mother knew exactly what he meant, as she had been holding Leslie in her arms at the time. (The incident had been responsible, in no small way, for her having become Mrs. Sturdley.)

Berman's harsh voice cut into the vacuum that had filled the room.

"So would you please still explain to me, somebody, how come we're cashing in more ——— coupons than we're printing?"

There was silence for a moment. The staff shuffled its feet in an erratic rhythm. "Tell him," Leslie managed to say to one of his assistants. "You had better tell him," the assistant replied.

"Can you tell me, Morris?" said Berman gently.

"I think there's something wrong, Sol," said Morris.

"Can anybody tell me how we're getting back more than we're sending out?"

"Tell him," Leslie whispered to one of his associates.

"No, you tell him, Mr. Onandorfer," came the answer.

"Somebody tell me how," said Berman, taking a long breath. "SOMEBODY TELL ME HOW!"

11 How the Beans Were Spilled and Oliver Felt His Oats

Last night, the Acropolis Repertory Theatre presented a revival of the Sophocles tragedy *Oedipus Rex* at the One Flight Down Theatre in the basement of P.S. 91. The kindest thing I can say in connection with this production is that the director, a twenty-two-year-old Romanian actor, must be suffering from an acute Freud complex.

Not bad at all, George Revere was thinking as he pored over his review of the previous night's opening in lower Manhattan. He sat at his desk in the Alarum Building, his feet braced against the lower-right-hand drawer of his desk, the morning paper open on his lap.

The translation was notable only for its rendering of the blind Oedipus' first line as "Horrors! I can't see where I'm going or hear what I'm saying," surely the worst paraphrase of its type outside of movie subtitles. Forgoing the traditional Greek masks, all of the actors played under layers of clown white so thick that they looked like animated *charlottes russes*—their voices bubbled disagreeably through the pastry with all the expression of waves slapping against a rowboat.

Damn, there I go with the makeup again, George thought. He hoped Conklin hadn't noticed. Skipping to the last paragraph, he skimmed through his coda:

Greek civilization had withstood many bludg-
eonings in history; I expect it will survive last
night's production. I can only add that next to the
disaster at the One Flight Down Theatre, Oedipus'
misfortune takes on the emotional magnitude of a
lost collar button. The most charitable thing I can
do at this point is to ignore the hapless actors and
technicians who have become enmeshed in this
atrocity and hope that they, thus clothed in welcome anonymity, will be encouraged to collect
their Equity minimum and desert the foundering
ship.

Perhaps the last sentence had become a little too involved in beating the point to death, but George felt
reasonably well pleased with the overall effect. He did
not completely realize what was happening to him.
Within the past few weeks his reviews had changed
from polite (or, at the most, impolite) little telephone-
book reviews (in which everyone is listed and few opinions are expressed) to deeply committed comments on
the life that exists between the first-act rise and the
final-act drop.

George Revere was beginning to appreciate the
Theater.

Heretofore he could completely fail to understand the
compulsion of adults to make-believe in public and
could titter inwardly at the spectacle of other adults
beating their hands together at the presentation of a
false world. Now an insidious change was taking place.
It had started slowly. First, he had written an entire notice without mentioning makeup. This milestone went
unremarked. On another occasion he had completely
forgotten what the set had looked like. He put it down
to dyspepsia.

Then, another strange feeling had overtaken him. He
no longer plodded through his confined universe, inex-
tricably nailed by each footstep to the concrete sidewalk
below him. He moved absentmindedly, as through a

dream. His eyes seemed to be focused through the confusing lens of unreality. The buildings and storefronts he knew so well suddenly became suffused with a strangeness he could not place. He was living in a world made of Celotex and canvas, a city and a life from which the substance had been drained away and time became a succession of magic-lantern slides.

It is a hard sensation to describe. It is as if you have been away for months, years, from a home you once knew intimately: everything is the same, but nothing is quite right; the home has become so perfectly true in relation to your thoughts and memories that the entire idea of *this home* becomes false. It is the falseness of the theater, the truth of the drama.

This had all come about, imperceptibly, because of a grain of knowledge that George had brought back with him from Central Park; transplanted into his everyday life, it had grown in two weeks to cover everything with a soft, gauzy film of fallacy.

In this topsy-turvy atmosphere of a life gone motley, George not unnaturally felt himself drawn to the truth of its representation on a stage; he became one with the performances and began writing thoughtful criticism from his vantage point on the inside looking in. His review of *Oedipus* was a typical symptom; shocked and cheated by its falseness to art (which has little, if anything, to do with falseness to life), he had attacked it violently as a personal imposition on his own sensibilities.

The separation of true art from false life has marked the transition of many reviewers to critics. George was not immune.

"All right, Georgie, wake up. It's time to go home."

George looked up from his paper, startled. Ross stood over him, a large grin on his face.

"If you're still savoring the hatchet job you did on the Greek thing last night, you should be ashamed of yourself. Conklin tells me the backers will probably be streaming in here with warrants and horsewhips any minute."

"If anybody put any money into that stinker, it was either out of hatred of theatergoers or a desire to write it off as an income-tax deduction."

"Hey, wait a minute," said Ross. "You don't have to convert me. I'm just playing. Anyway, it's time to pop off."

George looked at his watch. "I think I'm going to hang around for a while, Stuie."

"Making points?"

"No, I have a show later on, and I don't feel like fighting the crowds going uptown now, just so I can fight them coming back downtown later. I think I'll stick around here. I'll send Pete down for a couple of hamburgers in a while."

"Another Little Theatre effort?"

"Yeah."

"Shakespeare?"

"Not this time. It's not *The Drunkard* either, but it's almost as bad. A revival of *East Lynne*. There's a thought to bring a lump to the pit of your stomach."

"Well, good luck, Georgie. Oh, and be sure to pick up a copy of tomorrow's rag before you leave—I've got a surprise for you."

"A surprise." George was startled by Ross's air of complicity. "What the hell kind of surprise?"

"You'll see," said Ross. "Enjoy your hamburgers. Tonight *East Lynne*."

"Oh, God," groaned George, "don't remind me."

"Do not despair," chuckled Ross. "Keep the hatchet sharp and the bludgeon blunt, and one of these days you may be front and center at a real theater instead of a converted railroad flat."

"So long, Stuie."

"See you. Don't forget to pick up the morning edition."

"Give me a hint?"

"Nope. See you tomorrow."

With a wave, Ross ambled out of the office, leaving George sprawled in front of his littered desk staring malevolently at two tickets for that night's opening. He had not told Ross that another reason he dreaded the play was the fact that he would be there alone—the new receptionist had developed an ingrown toenail just after lunch, and George had been unable to find anyone who wanted to take a chance on *East Lynne* with him. He was not only disturbed by the jibes that would be thrown his way by his opposite numbers on the other sheets—Rathborn would bring that dancer he's been living with, George was sure, and Rogers would probably escort the same blond teenage delinquent who would always be pinching him in the dark—but George had noticed that he was becoming increasingly nervous about being alone at any time. Even in his own apartment, he would feel a sense of emptiness, of strangeness, unless he had someone he could talk to or, at least, be with. He had taken to watching television until the point of exhaustion and would only drag himself to bed between *The Night Show* and *The Dawn Show,* or simply fall asleep on the sofa.

He stared at the offending tickets again. The idea of an ingrown toenail haunted him. He had never thought of that particular complaint as ever constituting an emergency, but anyway, he thought, it was a lot more original than a headache.

Dinnertime came and went; so did Pete, the office boy, with George's double hamburger and coffee. George worked slowly on a small piece he was doing for Features on fishing in the Hudson River. The idea bored him; he was repelled by the thought of eating the products of a river whose stock of maritime and industrial wastes never ceased to fascinate him when seen from pierside. At about eight o'clock he began to clean off his desk; one ticket went into the wastebasket and the other into his coat pocket. Before he left, the memory of Ross's promised surprise drew him to the corner of the small room where the long galley proofs dangled limply over the checker's table. He riffled through the yellow sheets looking for the feature pages.

They found him.

Bannered across Ross's first page, in bold type, was the line:

CENTRAL PARK RENEGADES
LIVE ON TRADING STAMPS!!

and the byline read: Stuart Ross and George Revere.

Oh, my God, thought George over and over again, *Oh, my God.* It was mostly all there, even some details he had forgotten but which Ross, with his reporter's memory and nerve, had recalled. True, several choice items were missing—the hijacking of auto batteries, for instance, and El Greco's curious hobby. But there was little comfort to George in these omissions; he sensed Ross's desire for follow-up material. In fact, the story ended with a slug promising further installments. George was numb. The tiny grain that had been germinating in his mind suddenly burst; the distorted lens through which he had been recently viewing the world was the Park Place, and his sense of disquiet was a bad case of Lynnlessness.

He dashed to the nearest telephone and nearly dislocated a forefinger dialing.

"Hello?"

"Ross, you bastard, is this your idea of a joke?"

On the other end of the line, safe by half an island, Stuie Ross beamed. "No, you idiot. The story is running in the next four issues as a serial, and Conklin is pushing you up to assistant features."

"And what are you getting out of it?"

"Sunday magazine."

George was suddenly furious. "Goddamn it, Stuie, I thought I told you I didn't want any of this in print. It's a lousy thing to do."

Ross seemed surprised. "Are you still feeling sorry

for those renegade gypsies? George, I thought you had come back to the living."

"Renegade, renegade. You're talking like your own headlines. Damn it, I think it stinks." George was close to violence.

"Sorry, George, but a good story is a good story. I gave you billing, anyway. Go see *East Lynne* and sleep on it. It's probably the best thing that's happened to you since you ran into me in Central Park last month."

Not knowing what to say, George jammed the phone down into its cradle and stood for a moment transfixed. The small room was deserted; there was only the constant background sound of the teletypes spewing out news by the foot, news by the yard, news by the mile. All time seemed to halt, except for the time on George's wristwatch, the time on the wall, and the time of the teletype with its cicadalike rumble.

Eight-twelve, eight-thirteen, eight-fourteen. At nine o'clock the trucks would start to roll. At nine-twenty the first deliveries would start. At nine-twenty-five the first sales would be made. At nine-thirty . . . What?

"Pete. Pete! PETE!!" screamed George through the open door.

"Yes, sir." The office boy was running to him from across the floor. George began to run to meet him.

"Listen closely, Peter. Here is a ticket to a show that starts in a half-hour. There's another one in my wastebasket. Take your mother. Take your wife, if you've got one. Take someone else's wife. GO TO THAT SHOW! Get me a program and call me when it's over. If I'm not home, keep calling me until I get home, even if it isn't for a month. Understand?"

The two of them were running side by side toward the elevator.

"Yes, sir," said Pete, "but—"

"No buts," shouted George as the elevator doors closed. "If you don't get to that play, I'll have your—"

The descending elevator cut off the word "job," but George's meaning was clear. Pete dashed off to find the other ticket, and George plunged out into the rain to find a taxi.

A great deal has been written about the game of finding taxicabs in New York during a rainstorm. There is little or no necessity for another such essay, except, perhaps, to remark that due to certain minuscule fluctuations in the relative humidity, imperceptible even to the United States Weather Bureau, taxicab drivers in New York can sense rain. And since everyone should know at least enough to come in out of it, the New York cabdriver, responding to this meteorological alarm, cranks up his windows, locks his doors, puts his flag up and his *OFF DUTY* sign on and beelines it back to the nearest shelter that can be termed a garage. This may easily turn out to be Monaghan's Bar, Grill, and Garage on upper Third Avenue, where a storm of any length can be waited out; the distinction is lost on the wet, angry, exhausted pedestrian who stands in the middle of a cross street waving his arms while the rain pours down his neck from the rim of his hat and two cabs race by in tandem, their drivers staring fixedly ahead.

A great deal has been written in this vein, but George still managed to catch a taxi on the third try. (The driver happened to be heading in the same direction, anyway.)

"Take me up the West Drive in the Park to about Eightieth Street—I'll let you know where I want to get out. and hurry."

"Sure," said the driver, who was hoping he could get to Monaghan's before a downtown or, worse, a Brooklyn fare caught him in an unguarded moment. The cab flashed through the rain-streaked night; the city was a frosted abstract of colored and brightly lit blobs on the windows. George sat back in the pleasantly dank interior of the taxi and tried not to think about what might be happening in the Park. He looked at his watch. Eight-thirty-six. He cleared a small arc on the steamy window nearest him: the wet, black streets reflected the buildings and lights back at him; a steady stream of cars sped past in the opposite direction, scattering the large rain drops. The sounds of traffic muted to a continuous *swish* of rubber in water. George looked again. They were turning down Sixtieth from Park Avenue; in the distance he could see the shimmering reflections of red stop lights at Fifth awaiting them.

The Park swept away to his right, a dark, indistinct blur in the channels of light that crisscrossed the remainder of his vision. The windshield wipers drummed their metronomic beat, ticking away the interminable minutes as the light stayed red . . . and red . . . and red.

"It's a long light," mumbled George uncomfortably.

The driver turned around with an open smile, as if inviting camaraderie. "Sure is. But if you think this one is long, boy, you should have ever seen the Old Ocean Parkway lights in Brooklyn. Talk about long lights. I useta go out of my way to catch up to a green section when I was crossing—they useta work in blocks of five, ten lights, you know—I useta go outa my way, like I said, to—"

"It's green," cried George desperately, and a horn blast just behind them italicized his words. "Go ahead."

The driver's face froze at this blatant breach of friendly conversational etiquette. "Sure, sure, mister. Take it easy."

The cab leaped forward, throwing George back into the cushioned seat, and immediately stalled. George heard the driver curse once and then grind the starter ineffectually. The horn blast to their rear was repeated with more insistence; the tune was quickly taken up, *a cappella*, by an increasing chorus of protesting voices.

"Ah, shaddap," the driver shouted out of the window, but this comment only seemed to rouse the horns to greater frenzies of caroling. Within a few seconds the pattern had been set: the car directly behind them would introduce the melody—a short monotonic phrase—which would be taken up by the contraltos, sopranos (perhaps a sports car), and a bass (Railway

Express) in a complex rhythmical pattern of fugue and counterpoint.

"Ah, shad*dap!*" the driver yelled again; he was obviously no music lover.

Under this din, the motif of the cab's starter, endlessly grinding the engine, without the slightest sign of creating the necessary spark of life, served to drive the accompanying horns to new heights of achievement.

"Baaaahh," sang the car behind.

"Buroop, buroop," chimed in Railway Express.

"Bedeep, bedeep, bedeep," lilted the sports car.

"Arooga," faintly intoned an unknown participant from halfway down the block.

"Rrrrr, Rrrrr, Rrrr," answered the cab.

"Baaah buroop bedeep buroop rrrrrr bedeep buroop rrrrrr bedeep arooga."

It was quite exciting. George nearly jumped out of his skin.

"What the matter? What is it? I've got to be there." Eight-forty-five.

"Relax, brother. If she starts, you get there. If not, you walk. Ya want me to carry you on my back?"

"Rrrrr arooga bedeep rrrrr buroop bedeep."

George felt himself breaking out in a film of sweat. The traffic light changed monotonously from green to red again. He reached into his pocket and brought up a crumpled dollar bill, which he thrust over the front seat.

"Here," he said breathlessly, "this is far enough."

The driver took the bill laconically. "As you wish," he said as George yanked open the door and slithered out into the wet street. The sound was clearer in the open air; a small crowd had gathered for the concert.

"Bedeep bedeep buroop rrrrr agrooga bedeep baaaahh."

George shruddered and ran jerkily across Fifth Avenue, searching in vain for the sight of another taxi. The rain had eased off slightly; a fine mist of water hung over the city, blowing to and fro with every vagrant breath of air. The lights threw their diffuse haloed beams of yellow, red, and green in all directions. Only the Park, lying quiet and black in the nighttime clamor, seemed immune from the crazy quilt of submarine activity that is New York on a rainy night.

A taxi dashed across Fifty-ninth Street and down Fifth. Yelling, George ran into the street, causing an oncoming car to squeal to a sudden stop. He jumped back to safety as the cab faded into the distance.

Nine-oh-three. The trucks had begun to roll.

George could have screamed with exasperation. He thought of commandeering an automobile. A quick leap to the running board, a crisp "Follow that car." No running board. He darted halfway down the street, thinking about a fast mile-and-a-half run to the Place. Four minutes to a mile? Six minutes for a mile and a half. He darted back to the corner in time to wave impotently at a taxi's receding taillights.

Nine-ten.

That was when George saw the horse.

This particular horse did not just happen to materialize on a whim at this point in time; if George had looked carefully, he would have seen the horse before. In fact, he had had almost seven years of chances to see this particular horse on this particular corner, since that was the length of time it had been calling the Plaza home.

The horse was old and tired, attached through necessity, birth, and harnessing to an equally old and tired hansom cab. Although many such cabs are generally in evidence when the weather may be counted on to attract young lovers and/or elderly vice-presidents with their secretaries, tonight only this one hansom braved the suspended wetness of the summer drizzle. It was a closed cab, and George could see, by the crown of a top hat that was the Central Park driver's badge of office, that its owner was inside, taking advantage of his rank while his horse stood patiently outside.

Why not?

George rapped on the door of the cab until the driver

peered through the window. "How much?" George asked.

"On the side," said the driver cryptically, and like Alice's caterpillar, disappeared.

George looked on the other side of the cab where the rates were printed in fading numbers. They sounded reasonable. He knocked again. This time the driver, sensing a fare, came down the stairs. "Where to?" he said.

"West Drive in the Park to about Eightieth. I'm going to Belvedere Tower."

"I can get closer on the Transverse."

"OK," said George. "Only hurry."

"You call it," said the driver. As George climbed into the cab, the driver mounted into his box and took the reins. "Away we go," he called.

City horses are not built for speed. They are built to move vegetables, stomp on rioters, or lull romantics into the nineteenth century. This is perhaps just as well: it would be ghastly to picture a collision between a galloping equine mass and the latest model from Detroit's tinworks. When the cheery "Away we go" reached it, the horse moved from the curb at an infinitesimal rate and inched into the protesting stream of traffic. At any other time, George would have found the swaying of the cab and the clipclop and steel on asphalt particularly relaxing; at the moment it was all he could do to keep from ripping the interior apart out of exasperation.

"Hey, doesn't this thing go any faster?" he called.

"Nope," came the answer. "Traffic's too heavy."

George sighed and dropped back into his seat. He stared out over the tops of the automobiles hurtling by him, each one reflecting the hansom crazily on its wet roof.

Nine-twenty-three. The deliveries had started.

The traffic continued unabated; looking out of the window, George could see a steady stream of cars sweeping into the Park from all sides. They would never have a chance.

"Hey," he called up to the driver.

"Yeah?" came the returning monosyllable.

"I'm in a real hurry. I've got to make it to the Tower in the next five minutes."

"Can't do it."

"I'll make it worth your while."

"Make it worth Oliver's while."

"Who the hell is Oliver?"

"Horse."

George looked out desperately at Oliver. Oliver's head drooped, his back swayed, and his tail swished as he plodded uncaringly, unseeingly through the tangle of strange, shiny, evil-smelling little monsters all around him. What he needed was an unobstructed road and a touch of the whip, George decided. An unobstructed road . . .

"Hey," he called again.

"Yeah?"

"Take it up the bridle path."

There was a stunned silence.

"What was that?"

"I said drive up the bridle path, and give Oliver his head. I'll make it worth both your whiles."

Finally George had provoked a reaction from the driver, who dropped the reins and leaned down to talk. Oliver kept plodding away down Fifty-ninth Street—he should have gone into business for himself, George thought; the driver seemed to be completely superfluous.

"Mister," said the driver, "my while is worth a damn sight lot more than you can pay me if it means trouble with the fuzz. They'll take my hack license away."

"Tell them Oliver got uppity and ran away."

"They'd fine me."

"How much?"

The cabbie took off the top hat and scratched his woolly hair. "Hard to say. Twenty, twenty-five bucks."

"Here's thirty bucks," said George. "Open Oliver up on the bridle path."

"I'll never make it," said the driver uncertainly.

George felt he was winning; now they were at least haggling about price. "Thirty-five bucks. Pull her up onto the path. We'll be lost in the Park before we can be spotted."

"Let's have the money."

George counted out three tens and a five and passed them up to the driver. "This is gonna be a shock to Oliver, but here we go!"

He drove the horse into a gap in traffic and then pulled lightly on the reins. Oliver immediately assumed that it was either a mistake or that his master was trying to catch a glimpse of some advance necking in the cab below. He did not respond. The driver pulled harder and flicked Oliver with the crop. Surprised and hurt, Oliver stopped and looked up at him reproachfully.

"Go on, you nag," shouted George. "I've got thirty-five bucks riding on you."

A lifelong racehorse would not have responded as well even to a reverse in parimutuel odds: Oliver suddenly mounted the curb, and with the cab following closely, sprang into a delighted canter down the bridle path.

"Thattaboy," cried the driver, exalted by this unexpected airing. "Gidyap."

Two elderly women, who were walking briskly past the Park, barely slowed their pace.

"What was that, Martha?" asked one.

"I suppose it's one of those happenings," said the other, and they left it at that.

George was ecstatic. The cab swayed precariously as Oliver plunged headlong down the cinder track. The feel of something besides asphalt under his hoofs had taken fifteen years off his age; he responded to the crop with a dashing exuberance which, though not quite worthy of a Sea Biscuit, was a good cut above the New York automotive average.

Nine-thirty-six. From somewhere off in the distance,

George thought he could hear a faint siren, rising and falling in the wet air like a circling horsefly.

"Faster," he shouted, "faster!"

If there had been any passersby that night, they would have had a story to tell which might have one day ranked Central Park with Sleepy Hollow in New York's folklore. Through the dim haze of the mist, just outside the scattered curtain of light thrown by the nearest feeble streetlamps, comes the pounding of hooves on the bridle path and the agitated screeching and rattling of a rushing conveyance. All at once the cab flies into view. On the box the driver stands precariously, a demonic look on his face as he shouts to his steed, lightly flicking his crop in the air. A solitary passenger in the cab is leaning dangerously out one window, urging the driver into even greater feats of speed. And in front of all, the horse; the horse is leaping along in an erratic gallop, his wide eyes staring out into the night between huge leather blinders.

Then, with a rumble and a cry, they are gone again into the mist—the phantom hansom and its cargo— leaving behind only a strange drumming in the earth and a beating in the spectators' hearts.

Nine-forty-one.

George clung to the door as the driver reined in, pulling Oliver to a trot and finally to a stop. Just over the rise George could see the Tower silhouetted dimly against the reddish night sky. He jumped onto the damp path and waved at the driver.

"Thanks, friend," he called. "You can get back on the road from here."

"Don't mention it," came the answer, and in another moment Oliver had wheeled around and was gone. George stood at the edge of the road for a second and then set off toward the Place at a run. He cut across the uneven ground, his feet sinking into the damp soil. Once he fell, but he jumped to his feet again and continued his crosscountry sprint. For a while he ran parallel to the roadway; then he struck off into the bushes, plunging forward through the wet, crackling branches and leaves, one hand in front of his face, his toes digging into the grass.

The siren appeared to be louder—the noise cut into George's consciousness with one result: *faster, faster . . .*

He crashed through the last row of hedges and dashed around the foot of the long flight of stone steps leading up to the parapet. A dozen more long strides and he was standing, breathlessly, in front of the door that he had never really forgotten. He lifted his hand and knocked the rhythmical signal that had become a part of him. Dum, dee, dee, dum, dum.

He had barely finished when he noticed that the door was slightly open. He quickly pushed his way into the blackness inside.

"Lynn?" he called uncertainly. "Sally?"

He fumbled for the light switch and found it; as it clicked he stood blinking in the glare.

The Place was deserted.

That they had left hurriedly, George had no real doubt. Dishes were stacked in the sink and there was still bedding on the cots. Everything else identifiable was gone: the typewriter, the clothing, the crystal ball, the pile of trading stamps in the corner, Lynn. He also had no doubt that they were gone; the fact that the door was so obviously open spoke for itself. He walked slowly through the room. He looked at the bed where he had regained consciousness as Sally cheerfully predicted his recovery, at the alcove where Lynn had first come to him that one splendid night. He ran his fingers over the table where they had eaten and laughed and talked.

But now there was no sound other than that of his feet scraping on the stone floor and the constant dripping outside. George could see, lying in the corner near the stove, a rain-damp copy of the *Alarum* flung open to a story he had no wish to look at again. *But they always leave around Labor Day,* he thought to himself.

Sally told me that. Yet he could not bring himself to pick up the newspaper, and so he missed seeing, underneath it, the previous day's edition with a neat hole where his column had been clipped out.

"You're all crazy," George said aloud, as much to himself as to those who were not present. "You're all crazy," he repeated more softly, this time mostly to himself. He moved back through the room, shut the lights, and carefully closed the door.

The dark isolation of night enveloped him once more; the dream vision returned to him. This time he recognized it for what it truly was. As he stared with terror at Ross's article in the *Alarum,* the false lens had shattered into a billion pieces; everything had become real and solid again.

Until now.

It was as if all the forces of nature had conspired at that moment to demonstrate the anguish of an empty solitude to him. He walked mechanically down the long winding path leading from the Tower; the blackness draped over the landscape like a velvet slipcover, and the dismal wetness of the haze formed an infinite succession of damp gauze curtains through which he had to pass. Even the Park sounds—the muted roar of traffic flowing through unseen roads and the background rumble of the crickets and tree frogs—sounded unreal and dispirited. Above, the tall trees cut irregular patches out of the glowing red sky; in the bright circles of the lamps, droplets of fine rain hung suspended.

Through all this George moved slowly, a homing instinct bringing him closer to the edge of the city. But something about the place, the time, had crept into the fringes of his consciousness; at a slight rustling sound behind him, he spun instantly around in enough time to see a blackjack describe a short arc past his left shoulder.

George jumped aside only to find himself peering into a tantalizingly familiar face. Under other circum-

stances he might have tried a hesitant introduction—it
did not look now as if this would be an auspicious start
at a conversation. Instead he kicked out sharply and felt
his toe glance crunchingly off a solid point in the vicinity of his antagonist's kneecap. The man gave a cry of
pain and staggered heavily, almost falling against
George. George, in turn, dodged and hit out blindly at
the off-balance stranger; the man, bowing to the whims
of Kismet and the fickleness of fate, slumped obligingly
to the pavement.

"George!"

George's skin seemed to hurtle skyward as he heard
the anguished call from behind. Suddenly it all clicked.
The name, the face, the voice. If he had been awakened
by Ross that day on the Mall, it was now as if he had
stepped under the first spray of the morning's cold
shower. He dodged quickly over the fallen form on the
path and drove an awkward roundhouse punch into the
shadows. The shadows were much more corporeal than
they looked; generating a concussion then sent little
shooting pains up George's arm from knuckles to shoulder, his fist connected with something wet, soft, brittle,
and (finally) extremely hard.

At the other end of this action, with a grunt of dis-
may, Herman Krugwerksch went crashing backward,
arms outstretched, into the thorny arms of the waiting
hedges. There was a crackling, tearing noise, a brief
thump, and then silence.

Things were looking up.

Inside George's apartment the sirens sounded faint and
far away. The oscillating whine had lost its penetrating
terror; it had become only a familiar part of the sound
of New York. George sat at his deak—the chair pushed
back and his feet on the edge of his overflowing wastebasket—trying to collect and arrange his emotions in
some kind of logical order.

Emotions are like any other impulse—too many con-
flicting ones can pull the most precisely balanced mech-

anism to pieces. George was no exception. Without commenting on the exact state of his balance, it would be safe to say that the catalog of emotions he had run through in the past two hours had been enough to reduce a Zen master to a state of quivering jelly. In quick succession, there had been:

> bewilderment,
> boredom,
> horror,
> anger,
> agony,
> frustration,
> irritation,
> exasperation,
> excitement,
> depression,
> fear,
> belligerence,
> triumph,

and now, bewilderment again.

Underlying this brilliant spectrum of instability, one fact loomed large. Lynn was gone and he would never know her reason for keeping him nameless. He realized now that they had not been involved in his original disaster; the voice he had just heard crying his own name still rang reminiscently in his ears. But what had they used him for? She had been to his apartment; Cuttleworth had told him that much. Why? And why had she gone through all his things? Somewhere, George felt, there had to be a gimmick. Could the two heaps he had just left for the police near the Place have had any connection with Sally, Freddy, and . . . Lynn, after all?

Lynn had probably forgotten him—why couldn't he forget, too? Why—

The jangling of the telephone pulled him swiftly out of this dead end. He reached over to lift the receiver, but the movement was too much for his balance, which had become precarious physically, as well as mentally, during the past few minutes. As he felt the chair sliding, George tried to straighten up; he only succeeded in kicking over the wastebasket before he and the chair crashed heavily to the floor, dragging the telephone along with them.

"Hello," crackled a voice at the other end. "Hello, goddamn it. What the hell is going on there? George?"

Sitting on the floor in the midst of a pile of papers with a chair and a telephone capsized alongside him, George found it hard to maintain his fury at Ross. However, he made a valiant attempt.

"Hang up, Ross," he growled, "you're polluting my telephone. I don't ever want to hear your ugly voice again."

"Oh, come off it, George. Look, I'm sorry. I thought you'd be pleased."

"Pleased? You old hypocrite. You didn't give a damn what I thought, as long as you got the magazine assignment. A fine friend you turned out to be. A fine son of a bitch, that's what."

"Honestly, George. I didn't mean to throw you off the deep end. I didn't know these people still meant anything to you."

"I barely see what that has to do with it," said George, crossing his legs and switching the telephone to his uninjured hand. "I asked you a personal favor not to release this story, and what do I get? A five-column head and a byline on an article I didn't have anything to do with."

"And assistant features. Don't forget, you got assistant features, too."

"Features, hell!" George was playing absently with the contents of the wastepaper basket, examining the pieces one by one and dropping them back into the can. *Dear Sir: As you are obviously one of the fortunate few who would appreciate an offer of . . .* he read on one letter before he recrumpled it. On a slip of paper he saw

Valerie's telephone number; it took him a while to remember when he had written it down. He absently began to straighten another note.

"All right, George, so I'm a bastard. Look, I'll kill
the rest of the series. I'll tell Conklin we can't run the
rest, or something. It may mean my job, but we'll can it.
Maybe no harm's done. But, George, I'll be damned if
I can see what these gypsies have got over you. A
bunch of . . . George? George? Where the hell are
you?"

George was staring dazedly at the piece of notepaper
in his hand. He jumped up, the receiver still clutched in
his hand, and began to kick the rest of the litter under
his desk. All this time, he kept staring at the seven
words scrawled on the slip.

"George! What the ——— is going on there?"

George became aware of Ross's voice in his hand.
"Yeah, Stuie. Look, I'll call you back." He dropped the
phone with a crash; it lay sputtering near its overturned
base. He picked up the chair, righted it, and sat down
slowly, without taking his gaze from the note.

I love you, George Revere. Carmen Gitana.

He had found the missing double-six domino. *Where
is she now?* he thought excitedly. *How can I find her?
Where?*

Could there be a listing? An old listing from last season, perhaps? A new number? A clue? George ripped
open the classified telephone directory and tore through
the thick mass of yellow tissue-paper sheets. Gypsies,
gypsies, gypsies. No dice. Readers and advisers. Nothing.
What else, what else . . . Fortune-tellers! Of course.

The book perversely skipped from "Formal Wear
Renting" to "Forwarding—Freight." Mediums? Sorry,
wrong number.

George was about to give up in disgust when he had
one more flash of intuition. He flipped through the
pages hurriedly and ran his finger down the columns.
Then he cursed one short expressive curse and deliv-

ered the unoffending desk a kick that added a throbbing toe to the night's injuries. He had almost found what he was looking for—but not quite.

The classified stood open at the entry: "Palms—see Florists."

How Lynn Saw a Number and
         Sally Closed the Store

Sally Harmony sat stiffly in an old straight-backed chair, the seventy-eight cards of the tarot deck before her. On the other side of the narrow table sat a matronly, bluish-haired lady who clutched a mink stole tightly about her, even though the last week of summer was reasonably warm. But it was two weeks after Labor Day, and one wore a mink stole and one didn't wear white shoes.

Past the tarot deck, at one side of the table, stood a large glass sphere, in which a strange blue-gray light flickered rapidly, making the mink-stoled lady's hair seem even bluer in the reflection. A set of comfortable, homey curtains had been drawn across the storefront windows to shade the slanting late-afternoon sun; inside, the light was at a relaxing, carefully calculated level.

Sally reached for the deck of cards. Because her questioner was a woman, she conscientiously counted down to the eighth card from the top of the deck, removed it, and placed it face down in the center of the table. Then, taking up the remainder of the pile, she began to construct the ancient pattern of the *etteilla*. First she laid out the past—eleven cards in a line from the upper-right-hand corner of the table to a point directly in front of her that would become an apex of the triangle she was forming. The next eleven cards marched through the present in a line from the past to the glowing glass ball, passing under the intent eyes and slightly reddened nose of the lady in mink. Finally,

Sally completed the triangle with another eleven cards
running from the apex in front of her to join the last
card of the present—this was the future, and Sally
hoped for at least a few visually impressive cards; although it was easy to breathe significance into the num-
bered suit cards, the tarots themselves looked more
meaningful.

The store that Sally had rented for the winter was
one of her favorites. They had begun to move in soon
after the hot quiet of August had yielded to the renewed
metropolitan activity of September. The moving process
had been leisurely, an armload each evening, until the
moment, three nights before, when Mrs. Frisbey had
burst into the Place waving a fresh copy of the *Alarum*.
There had been little time for shock; after a half-hour
scramble, their few remaining portable possessions had
been gathered up and removed. The store's location, in
the East Forties, was not ideal, but could be counted on
for some before- and after-theater fallout from the west.
Its most desirable feature, from Sally's point of view,
was the bakery next door. The constant and tantalizing
odors of fresh bread, chocolate, and baking pies which
wafted through the connecting wall provided a constant
source of distraction to her clients and served the valuable purpose of covering up her inadequacies as a seer.
"Having a bakery next door is to fortune-telling what
driving a car is to radio—you may think you're listening
at the time, but later you're really left only with an impression. Whether it's a good or bad impression de-
pends only on you, and not on what you've been hearing," Sally would expound to anyone interested in her
rather abstruse theories on the mechanics of reading
and advising.

The front of the store was set up simply, in conform-
ance with another of her theories: that the gaudy and
ornate surroundings associated with gypsies only made
her clients nervous, and scared off many prospective
customers. She advocated the gray-flannel gypsy; a
man-of-distinction study would have suited her pur-

poses best of all, provided it was located next to a bakery. Behind a thin partition, peering through a small crack in the connecting door, Lynn Harmony watched her mother carefully deal out another series of thirty-three cards counterclockwise around the triangle and then place the last eleven under the first card in the center. The quavering light from the glass ball set out wan images in the slightly dimmed room.

" 'Double, double, toil and trouble; fire, burn; and caldron, bubble. Cool it with a baboon's blood, then the charm is firm and good,' " Lynn murmured as she inched the door shut and turned around. "He, he, he." Her sudden cackle startled Freddy, who was stretched out on one of the two beds poring over a seed catalog.

Lynn picked up her scrapbook and sat down on one of the small trunks they had not yet unpacked. Selecting a blank page, she reached into a pocket of her jeans and withdrew a crumpled square of newsprint. She stared at it with a mixture of interest and distaste, as an entomologist would regard a cockroach in his soup.

" 'Animated *charlottes russes*,' " she quoted quietly. "Always the makeup." She picked up the wrinkled clipping, and with a preoccupied gesture that seemed to divorce her hands from the rest of her body, tore it in half again and again, until the pieces were too small to grasp. Then she rose. The bits of newspaper floated down around her feet like a Lilliputian snowstorm.

Since the moment she had last seen George, high up on the rock outcropping at the base of the Tower, a qualitative change had seemed to come over Lynn's perception. Like a bathtub being emptied, something had twitched the plug, and she could feel the contents of her life draining—conditions in which she talked, thought, spoke, and dreamed were slowly changing in character. Not that they had become George-dependent. Even the newspaper article that had sped them out of the Place came as an anticlimax for Lynn. She looked around the room in which she was standing. Somehow it no longer had the trappings of glamour and mystery she associated with the long string of past stores—not even with this very one, in which they had lived twice before. All she could see was a fairly large room painted in a dull green made duller by a summer's worth of grime. Deep cracks branched out here and there on the walls, and flakes of brittle paint hung down from them like leaves from an off-color and demented tree. The rusty steam pipe slanted up from a jagged hole in the floor to a jagged hole in the ceiling, supporting a rickety shelf.

"I'm getting a reading from Mother's crystal," Lynn said suddenly, her eyes fixed on the shelf. A large glass globe, similar to the one in the front room, stood on the shelf, just above the level of Lynn's eyes, between a zodiac chart and a large shopping bag containing the last of their Royal Purple stamps.

"A reading?" Freddy tore himself away from an agonizing decision concerning Early Golden Summer Crookneck and Early Prolific Straightneck squash.

"Look." Lynn pointed at the globe. "One-five-eight-five-one-oh-four-three," she read off.

Freddy stood behind her, his stubby chin almost in her pony-tail, and tried to match her line of sight. "Oh, yeah," he muttered. "1585104 . . . 3," he made out, squinting.

They both turned around, to see where the reflection originated. The walls were bare, with the exception of Monet's *Four Poplars,* which El Greco had thumb-tacked to the plaster the previous night. The numbers seemed incorporeal, as if they had been generated within the glass.

Lynn saw it first. "The television," she said.

"Huh?"

"The TV," said Lynn. "It must be on the back of the TV set. See?"

An old television set stood against the rear wall, its back facing a wall mirror that had been left by some long-forgotten tenant. A glowing red light emanated from the set's back, indicating that it was in operation, but instead of a picture tube there was a gaping hole in the front of the cabinet, and several multicolored strands of wire trailed out through the hole and across the floor, disappearing under the partition between the two rooms. It was the picture tube, set into her table, that caused Sally's crystal ball to flicker.

Lynn crept behind the television and read off the serial number that, reflected in the mirror and the glass globe on the shelf, had startled her. "15851048," she said. "That's not quite right. What's the last number up there, Freddy?"

Freddy craned. "Looks like a three."

"Well, here it's an eight. But that's it, anyway." She came around to Freddy's side and stared at the crystal once more. "It does look like a three from here."

There was a moment of quiet as both stared up at the numbers with fierce concentration. "Boy, what a tip," murmured Freddy. "In the old days I would've blown a wad on that."

"What kind of a tip?"

"Oh, almost anything," said Freddy. "Numbers, eight-horse parley, turnstile counters, anything. About fifteen years ago I was coming around one of the corner ledges on the old Savoy Plaza—seventh or eighth floor, I don't really remember. Anyway, it's a good thing they tore that old pile down; those ledges were dangerous. So I was coming around the corner, when I ran into Digs Mochetti from Forest Hills coming along in the other direction. His pockets were stuffed with so much loot that it was all he could do to hang on with his toes. 'Hi, Digs,' I said. 'How's the pickings?' Well, Digs was real embarrassed, you know. Here I had taken the time to creep all the way around the building on one of the worst ledges in New York, and here he was coming back after having picked the floor clean. 'Hi, Freddy,' he said. 'Do you think you could move over and let me pass?' Well, I sure as hell didn't want to have to make it all the way back to the exit window and then have to come out again, but on the other hand, it looked like there might not be anything left to take, anyway. So I slipped under the ledge, holding on with my fingers, and motioned Digs on. 'Anything left, Digs?' I asked. 'Nope,' he said, and damned if he didn't come right down with his foot on my hand. Now, I'm pretty sure he didn't do it on purpose, but I was all set to scream something at him, when I looked up, and there, right on the bottom of his heel, I could see the number nineteen. Well, I knew they were off at Saratoga the next day, and this was too good a tip to lose. So as soon as Digs had edged past, I climbed up after him and beat it downtown to play the daily double on one and nine."

"And you won," said Lynn.

"Uh-uh," Freddy recalled, the fifteen-year-old loss still rankling. "No sooner did I get home than I began to worry about the number. I wasn't sure if I had remembered it right. So I called Digs the next morning and asked him to look at his right shoe and read me the number on the heel. Digs thought I had a screw loose, but he finally looked and said it was sixty-one. Sixty-one, see. Nineteen *upside down*. I had been reading him from underneath! So I got on the phone to Gus downtown, but it was too late. I was riding on one and nine."

"And six-one won."

"Yep." Freddy shook his head in amazement. "Paid six hundred and forty-four dollars and eighty-nine cents. I'll never forget that."

"Obviously," Lynn said.

"Anyway," Freddy finished, "it would be criminal to overlook a good tip like this, even though Sally wouldn't like it. The place to bet eight numbers today, I guess, would be the state lottery."

"You can't pick a number on that," objected Lynn. "You take what you get."

"I didn't mean from the State. A friend of mine over on Broadway uses the State's winner list but lets you pick your own number. He charges twice as much as the State, but makes the same payoff if you win."

"Really?" Lynn read the eight numbers from the crystal again, as if waiting for them to change.

"15851043." Then she walked over to the television and peered down behind it. "15851048. Well, which one do we play?"

"I don't know if we should. I don't go in for that sort of thing anymore."

"Why not? It's more than a tip. It's a last chance."

"We could play them both," suggested Freddy.

"No, that's against the rules."

"Hell it is. Hack's game is open to—"

"I didn't mean Hack's rules, or whatever his name is," said Lynn. She pirouetted gaily on the ball of her left foot, her hair flying around her like a golden propeller. "I mean the rules of the bigger game. We have to play this the way it's written for us, and we can't hedge our bets."

"Huh?"

"I say we bet the three. That's the number in the crystal ball. The other one's just the serial number of an old television set."

Freddy looked at the glass globe once again. The angle of the light was changing outside; he had difficulty making out the numbers. "Still looks like a three, all right," he said. "OK, we'll give it a try."

The sound of a chair scraping against the wood floor came from the front room. Lynn held up her hand.

"It sounds like Mother is finished with Mrs. Gorman," she said softly. "Not a word to her, now, about the lottery. She'll think it's insane."

Freddy was about to open his mouth to reply when the door to the front room opened and Sally swept in.

"What in the world was all that yakety-yak back here?" she demanded. "Luckily Mrs. Gorman thought it was coming from the bakery. How many times do I have to tell you that I must *concentrate*. I don't need quiet to be thoughtful, but I do need quiet to look thoughtful."

"Sorry," said Lynn. "I hope we didn't louse you up."

"No, not at all," Sally said. "Mrs. Gorman is worried about her investment counselor. Seems she's sure he's embezzling funds from her account or some such thing. I think I've convinced her that it's all in her imagination. After all, I figure that the chances are very good that he's not stealing a penny, but even if he is, she can still afford it. Knowing about it won't help her blood pressure. How are you, Freddy?"

"I—"

"Freddy has to go, don't you, Freddy? We'll see you later."

"But I—"

"Where are you off to?" asked Sally. "I thought you might help us finish unpacking."

"I don't—"

"Good-bye, Freddy," Lynn said gaily, taking him by the arm. "Hurry back."

They disappeared through the door. Sally sat on the bed and ran a hand through her short hair; when Lynn returned, she looked up quizzically.

"Now, what was that all about?"

Lynn perched on the trunk, her left leg folded underneath her.

"Look into your crystal ball and find out."

A frown mark etched itself above the bridge of Sally's nose. "Very funny," she said. "You win the hand-crocheted doily and get seventy-three on the laugh meter for that. Honestly, I understand your walking around all day as if you were going to be burned at the stake. I suppose we all go through that sooner or later. But it's the gallows humor—the brave-little-girl-on-the-scaffold attitude—that gets me. You don't have to put me on, dear. I understand."

"Do you?" Lynn appeared unconvinced. Her right foot swung back and forth, pendulumlike, ticking off the seconds. "We're in a dream, you know. Not a bad dream, but just a dream. A strange, meaningless, *floating* kind of dream. Everything is so *tentative*. Somehow I never seem to mind it as much in the summer, when we're at the Place. I know that should be the most un-real part of it, but it never seems that way. It seems more real, more solid, anyway, than these stores, and the fortune-telling. And now it looks as if we might not be able to get back to the Park next summer, and suddenly I feel as if I've had it."

"Yes, I know," murmured Sally. "And his name is George Revere."

Lynn sat up straight, startled, her foot frozen in time. Her only answer, when it finally came, was to dart past Sally and hurl herself onto her bed, sniffling. Sally leaned over and began to massage her neck carefully, with one hand, as if it were in danger of breaking. There was a look of distant pain on her face and in her eyes. "What we're going to do is this," she said firmly. "We've paid two months' rent on this store, and a month's security. About the middle of December, I will call your Aunt Geraldine in Clayville and I will tell her that we are coming home to Alabama for Christmas, if she will put us up in the proper holiday spirit. After that, we'll play it by ear. Maybe we can send you to the university. You can teach, and maybe I can get a secretary's job, and we can both rejoin society."

Lynn's shoulders shook and her voice, smothered in the pillow, cried, "That sounds awful!"

Sally nodded in agreement. "It does, rather, but we can't have it both ways. Either we're dream creatures or we're real, and Aunt Geraldine is the best idea I can think of right now."

Before Lynn could reply, there was a light rapping on the front door. It was El Greco, almost hidden behind several long rolls of canvas, which he deposited with reverence against a wall. He snorted when he saw Lynn crumpled on the bed.

"Now that your—*pfui*—boy friend has—what is it?—spilled the tables on us, I bring you more masterpieces to keep you company, to be safe. What is the world coming to when honest people are afraid of their shadows because of a yellow journalist, hey? For newsprint they sell their friends, no? Not even silver anymore." Greco's outrage could not be curbed by the warnings Sally flashed with her eyes, nor by Lynn's faint crying. "The newspaper is not Art. Art shows you how to feel, yes? The newspaper tells you what to think. Tomorrow, maybe, or the next day, someone picks up a paper, no? He reads about Greco in Central Park. Is it a work of Art that presents Greco to him? Does he feel what I feel? See what I mean? No! He reads this and that and thus and so, and it says what I do, and it tells him what to think about me, and Greco is gone. *Poof!* Greco will never exist to this newspaper reader except as a name and a reflex opinion. *Pah!* This is Art? No, *this* is Art!"

Greco stomped over to the corner and rapped his knuckles against the wall next to the Monet. "On the frame in the museum—in the jail—there is a brass plate under this that says 'Claude Monet. 1840-1926. *The Four Poplars*. 1891.' This brass plate is not Art, yes? It is like a newspaper. It tells you what to think. 'Monet, aha,' you say to yourself. 'Fine artist, no? Must be fine painting. Fifty-one when he painted it. Mature.' But here is the Art, right here, without the brass plate. It does not need the newspaper to say what it is. It *is*. The greens light up the room, no? The reds light up the world. What is wrong with the child, Sally?"

Sally, taken by surprise by Greco's abrupt change of subject, could only shrug and say, "A lot of things. Partly George, I guess." There was more snuffling from the bed, and Greco hmpfed.

"*Hmpf*," said El Greco. "There are two kinds of events in this world. One kind is forever, like the *Mona Lisa*. The other is for now, like whatever it is I'm sure your pretty little daughter is bawling about. If the *Mona Lisa* fell apart, I, too, would cry. If it is something like that, tell me, and I will cry with you, my dear. But if it is the other—for now—it is not worth tears, eh? It will be forgotten. Men still weep over the burning of the Alexandrian library, but how many centuries has it been since the last tear was shed over Helen's unfaithfulness?

Up, my child. Don't waste your precious tears on something of no consequence. You may use them all up, and then when you need them, they will be gone, no?"

There was much less noise issuing from Lynn, but Greco, carried away by his new-found role of comforter, swept on.

"I will tell you a story about those poplars," he said, gazing with something very like love at the blazing canvas on the wall. "Before Monet had a chance to finish that painting, he heard that the trees were to be sold for lumber. Would they wait until he was finished? No, no. Not where money was involved. *Pah!* They've got me over a barrel,' said Monet. 'If I try to bid on them, they'll take my last sou.' So he went to a local lumberman and said, 'Look. I want those trees, but only for a few months. You want them, but you don't need them right now. If you buy them, I will make up out of my own purse the difference between what you paid and what you would have been willing to bid in the first place.' So, 'Done,' cried the lumberman; and Monet got his painting, the lumberman got his wood, and we have . . . this!"

He turned toward the burst of blues, yellows, chartreuses, and lilacs. Lynn, drawn magnetically to the old man's tale, sat up on the bed, wiping away the dampness on her lower lids.

"Now, I ask you, which is the better Art?" demanded Greco. "The poplars on the river Epte, which are no longer there, the wood from the poplars, which probably went to make one of your newspapers, or Monet's poplars? Art follows Nature, eh? So where are the trees now?"

Sally looked amused. "But wasn't *Mona Lisa* painted on poplar wood?" she asked softly. Greco's eyes narrowed.

"I don't—" he began, but stopped. There was another rapping on the door, this time louder and more insistent. "I'll get it," said Sally and glided into the front room, leaving Greco uncharacteristically speechless and Lynn sitting on the edge of the bed, drooping like a well-wrung washingcloth.

Through the curtains on the front window Sally could see a tall man in the uniform of the New York Police. He stood stiffly in front of the door, one hand raised to knock again, the other resting on a rear pocket that was stuffed with what appeared to be enough in the way of notebooks, paper, forms, and writing implements to outfit a medium-sized grade school. He was looking up and down the street when Sally opened the door.

"Are you in charge here?" he asked.

Sally nodded, and he walked into the store. She closed the door behind him and took a deep breath.

"What's your name?" he asked.

"Sally Harmony."

"New here?"

"Not really," Sally said. "We were here at this address last winter. Officer Curso covered this neighborhood then."

"He's been transferred to the West Side," came the reply. "I'm Ryan. Who's 'we'?"

"My daughter and myself."

"And where have you been all summer?"

A frigid finger touched the small of Sally's back. "Visiting," she said. "Relatives. Out of town."

Ryan did not seem to be interested in pursuing the matter any further. He stood in the center of the room, staring suspiciously at the table with its crystal and its triangle of cards. "Are you a gypsy?"

"Partly," Sally lied.

"It's a good business."

Sally nodded imperceptibly, as if she had confirmed something in her own mind. "Since Officer Curso won't be able to take care of my donations to the fund," she said, picking up her handbag for the table, "I might just as well ask you to handle them for me."

"I don't know about any fund, but I do have some tickets for the policemen's ball left."

"I'll take two," said Sally promptly. "How much are—"

"You live here, too?" interrupted Ryan.

The cold finger behind Sally became a clammy hand. "Yes."

"Have permission?"

"Oh, yes," Sally replied. "I think I'll take four tickets, as long as you're here." She began to open her purse, but Ryan walked past her into the back room. Sally shrugged and followed him.

Lynn was on her feet again, standing near the rolls of canvas Greco had brought with him. The old man, eyes glinting behind his rickety glasses, was about to unroll one as Lynn watched. He stopped when Ryan and Sally came into the room, immobilized by the sight of the blue uniform and silver badge.

"My daughter, Lynn, and a friend, Mr. Kyriekides," said Sally formally. "Officer Ryan."

Ryan fixed El Greco with a stare that forced droplets of perspiration out of the old man's scalp. "You a painter?" he asked.

"I am an artist," said Greco. His momentary fright could never be so great that he would permit himself to be classed with any workman who wielded a paintbrush for a living.

Ryan grunted. "My wife paints. I've got lots of painters living in lofts on this beat. Nice kids. Do you live around here?"

The question took Greco by surprise. He started, and the roll of canvas almost dropped from his hands. Lynn caught it. There was a quick electric stillness; then Ryan, without waiting for an answer, strode across the room to the Monet. He stood in front of it and pushed the visor of his cap toward the top of his head.

"The trees are nice, but the colors are wrong," he commented. "Is this yours?" he asked, bringing his stare around to Greco again.

"Yes, it is," said Lynn quickly, afraid that the old artist's aphasia had reached the point at which even the

Hardy Boys would have detected something suspicious in it. But Ryan had returned to the Monet.

"At least I can see trees," he said. "Some of the stuff I see on the beat . . ." He shook his head and turned to face his captive audience again. Lynn clutched the canvas she had taken from Greco. Greco plucked nervously at the buttons on his corduroy jacket and looked appealingly at Sally. Sally held her open handbag in front of her like a shield, a smile fixed on her face.

"Are those your paintings, too?" Ryan asked, pointing at the canvas cylinders. "Can I see one?" he added, even before the artist had a chance to nod helplessly. Greco took the canvas Lynn was holding and unrolled it gently with reverently on the floor. It was Vermeer's *Young Lady with a Water Jug*. There was a moment of silence.

"I like that a lot better," said Ryan finally. "What's she doing with her other hand—the one out the window?"

"How should I—" began Greco, but thought better of it. Fighting down his twin hostilities to artistic illiterates and the police, he murmured, "She's watering a windowbox full of flowers."

"You should have shown them," Ryan said. "Anyway, what do you get for one of these?" he asked with a casual air meant to indicate that if the price was right he might be induced, someday, to buy a painting like one of the ones he had been shown. Greco swallowed.

"A thousand, fifteen hundred dollars," he replied. Sally crossed her fingers behind her back. There was no need to worry, however, because Ryan was clearly startled. "That's expensive," he said. "Do you sell many?"

"My works hang in the museum," said Greco.

Ryan looked impressed. He glanced again at the Vermeer and at the Monet, then turned to Sally. "Well, it was a pleasure meeting all of you. Did you say five tickets? They're two dollars apiece."

"Just fine," Sally said with relief. She transferred a folded bill from her purse to Ryan's extended hand. Ryan reached into his overflowing hip pocket and produced a creased wallet, in which he stowed the money.

"I expect you'll all be keeping your noses clean," he said in parting. "I'll be in from time to time." He squared off his cap and examined the Vermeer for the last time. "I still like that one on the floor better than the one on the wall," he said to Greco. "Well, good luck." Sally followed him out.

Lynn took a deep breath, as if the policeman had used up all the oxygen in the room just by his presence. Greco wiped his damp fringe of hair with one hand and muttered, "That was close, yes?" Lynn's answer was to abruptly stamp her foot, sending thin linear clouds of dust into the air from between the scarred floorboards.

"Yes, indeed," she exclaimed in a low voice. "And I say the hell with it. Mother and I are going back home next month, Greco. Or the month after. To Alabama. You can help us celebrate. Give Officer Ryan my regards, and Mrs. Frisbey, too, but I'm tired of *A Midsummer Night's Dream*. Everything is getting too close, and I don't need it."

Lynn paused for breath and slowly turned around, her gaze sweeping the room before her. Monet's poplars glistened on the wall in the last fading light of the sun, which was disappearing behind the apartment building on the other side of the courtyard. El Greco's rumpled face was concerned, and his hands, palms out, were slightly extended toward Lynn, offering only puzzlement. On the high shelf, Sally's crystal ball caught a corner of the light as the fugitive number in its interior dimmed out; from where Lynn stood, the glass reflected only the bag containing the now useless sheets of trading stamps. Vermeer's young lady smiled straight up from the floor at the cracked ceiling, one arm held permanently out the window in her never-to-be-fathomed gesture. Freddy's seed catalog lay on the bed, its pages open to a King of the North green pepper (early, prolific). And on the floor near her feet were the shredded remnants of a newspaper clipping, like the forlorn confetti of another year's party.

"I don't need it," Lynn repeated, and she could feel her throat tightening. "You're all crazy!" she whispered and once more flung herself on the bed, crying fiercely.

It was brighter in the front of the store: the late-afternoon sun still sparkled in the street outside. Ryan's blue form passed through the doorway like an eclipse. *What was it that I was searching for in New York thirty years ago?* Sally thought to herself as she watched his uniformed back receding down the street. She was about to swing the door shut when she saw another figure pass the policeman near the corner, walking slowly up the street toward the store. It was George Revere, hands in pockets, eyes surveying both sides of the street as he strolled. Sally's lips tightened. Sure she was unseen, she closed the door and flipped over the rectangular cardboard sign which hung against the glass. The side that said "Reader and Adviser—Come In" faced her now; from the outside the sign would read "MOVED."

She drew back a corner of the window curtain and watched, held by the inevitability of George's progress up the street. As he came abreast of the store, he stopped; Sally knew he was looking at the palmistry charts and dream-reading books piled in the other window. He had changed little in the past two weeks: he was wearing a fairly well-tailored gray summer suit instead of Freddy's old jacket, and the visible signs of the blow he had received on the back of his head had disappeared. But his manner was still hesitant; on his face Sally could still discern the existence of a quest. *Not his name*, she thought. *What, then?* She watched him stand for a moment, examining the MOVED sign; for that brief period of time she could have reached out and touched him, had the dusty plate glass, turned by the sun into a one-way window, not been there. Instead, she continued to watch him as he reached into his pocket for a notebook and wrote something down with a small pencil. Then he continued on his way and passed out of her line of sight.

Without showing any additional expression, Sally dropped the curtain and returned to the back room. The subdued sounds of Lynn's sobbing and Greco's consolation floated out to meet her, mixed with the tempting odor of lemon meringue.

13 *How Autumn Came to New York*

The discovery of one reader and adviser who appeared to be no longer in storefront residence had very little impact on George Revere. He strolled on toward the avenue, secure in his knowledge that there were plenty more where that one had come from and that the chances of this having been the right one were correspondingly slim. Nevertheless, he made a note to try again, and continued his exploration.

The end of September ushers in one of New York's two fleeting annual periods of glory. Together with late spring these crisp, clear days, comprising some six weeks in all, manage to make up for at least three hundred and twenty days a year of blast-furnace heat, bone-chilling cold, rainforest precipitation, and an atmosphere consisting of nine parts of carbon monoxide, sulfur fumes, and soot to every one part of air. The end of September and the bulk of October, like the crystalline month of May, bring to New York a hint of life in the perfect city; the glittering concrete and glass angularities of a thousand buildings carve channels across the island from horizon to horizon, as far as the eye can see. The impression is one of excitement. Everything is opening, closing, starting, stopping, going, coming, rising, falling simultaneously. And all over Manhattan people begin to circulate earlier in the morning and to spend days in aimless strolling and window-shopping.

For the past week George Revere had joined the crowds of walkers, circlers, millers, and plodders. However, George was not strolling aimlessly—he had a purpose. He was having his fortune told. And told. And told.

George had never noticed, in his pre-Park existence, the great number or many locations of readers and advisers, so called, in the city. Now it seemed as if half the city's population made a living with the crystal ball and the tarots. It was a difficulty he had not expected.

The first thing he had learned from his quest was that it was not propitious to ask for Lynn and Sally Harmony. Without a flicker of recognition, the proprietresses of the little stores tucked in unlikely corners of the island would find his palm immediately clouding over with grim predictions of trouble. Whether they knew Lynn and Sally or not, George decided, they were not going to give out any information that was not recorded in his lifeline. He then became more roundabout, saving himself from being the target of so many depressing preditions; still, the general pattern of his visits, and the answers they elicited, remained about the same.

He would stroll down a side street, alert for a curtained store window framing a small potted plant and crude sign. A bell would tinkle as he walked in; the reader and adviser would come out from a back room, sit down, and proceed to determine the answers that would be expected of her. George had learned to be extremely helpful during these interviews; he freely dropped clues about his profession, his marital status, his boyhood, and various other problems into her burgeoning script. In the meantime, he would plant a few remarks about his inquiry and let them germinate.

The results hardly varied. After a polite, formal session, which invariably sounded like one of Sally's tapes, he would be ushered out with a nod, a smile, a dream book, and no further information. His only chance, he decided, was to stumble upon the Harmonys *chez Gitana*, but the chance of realizing that goal was rapidly approaching the probability associated with locating one particular Mr. Jackson, whose first name was unknown ("We always called him Jack"), in the Manhattan telephone directory.

After a week of eliciting this kind of response during his lunch hours, evenings, and other available moments, George was beginning to feel that his was a hopeless cause. The fact that at any given moment he was only within five or ten miles of Lynn Harmony and could not bridge that distance was vastly frustrating to him. *Anyway*, he rationalized, *they probably never want to see me again, after having read that damn newspaper article. But*, the answer would come, *I could explain. I could explain.*

He walked disconsolately down a nondescript street in the East Thirties under rows of grimy warehouse and loft windows. It had been another fruitless lunchtime, in which, with a hamburger and a Dr. Pepper in his hand, he had explored a five-square-block area south of the Alarum Building. He had flushed three readers without luck. He kicked at a pebble on the sidewalk and moved on past a particularly forbidding structure from whose castiron facade peeling flakes of paint drifted down to the street.

It was too bad that George, as he passed, could not have overheard a conversation that was going on only some fifty feet over his head at that moment. If his hearing had been considerably more acute, or his curiosity more shameless, he could have peered up through the row of almost opaque windows, just above the sign that read faintly "Royal Purple Building," and listened in.

"Aha," Sol Berman was screaming at a shaken, ashen Leslie Onandorfer. "Aha, you assassin. I need my wife's aunt should have to tell me I'm being swindled? Friday, she says to my wife, 'Wasn't that a funny article about all those cute gypsies forging your stamps. I hope you didn't lose much money.' And where was I when she was reading this? I ask you, assassin. Wasn't I here trying to understand how we were doing more business than was possible? Hah?"

Lesile felt strangely deserted without at least one multi-colored chart behind him to which he could turn for moral support. It had been a bad few days for him, ever since he had seen the *Alarum* article; he had spent the interim hoping and praying that neither Berman nor any conceivable acquaintance of Berman's had been reading the features section that fateful day.

A reporter had actually called him for more information; with his heart somewhere in the vicinity of his pharynx, he had refused comment. For the next day or two he had scanned the paper in vain for a continuation of the dismal story; when Thursday came and went without a word, he began to breathe more freely. It was as if a providential patron saint of Onandorfers had wiped the slate clean and killed the story. Leslie never suspected that it was one of the demonic writers of the article, St. George Revere, who had been his temporary savior. Now he stood in the dock, facing the apoplectic rage of his boss. From the moment shortly before, when the intercom had crackled, "Onondaga, two minutes!" he had known the jig was up.

"Murderers! My heart! A million coupons don't grow outa nothing, Onondaga. They grew outa your head. That's worse than nothing. That's *absolutely* nothing. Oh, oh!"

Berman slumped back in his chair, feebly waving a copy of the offending newspaper in front of him. Words seemed almost to have failed him, but he rallied admirably.

"Little red lines running up and down charts I need to tell me, yet. What do they tell me, Onondaga? I'll tell you what they tell me. They tell me that I'm a goddamn' fool for thinking that a guy without pushcart experience could run a business! God help the FBI, Onondaga, if you were working for the Treasury Department."

"I—I—" Leslie put in, strangling on the hopelessness of it all.

"Yai, yai, yai," mimicked Berman. " 'Please, Mr. Hoover, it's the redemption of the pituitary dividends that's causing the fiscal increase to be received at our banks. It's the cause and effect of the new bond-interest capitalization.' And you know what, Onondaga? Hoover would say to you just what I'm going to say to you now, Onondaga. You're fired! Get out of here before I can see you again. You can go back to Columbia and teach your red lines, for all I care, but you're through in the coupon business. I never liked your name anyway. It sounds like an Indian."

Leslie backed dazedly to the door as Berman waved him off wearily, like a man flicking a june bug off his lapel.

"I—I never thought—Mr. Berman—"

Berman looked up sharply. "Exactly, Onondaga. So go back to the last of the Mohicans, where you came from."

He buzzed Morris on the intercom, hoping that the two of them might be able to compute the damages. After all, Morris was still a man with experience, even if he was a relative of his wife's.

George never remembered just when the Idea struck him. It may have been when Conklin came over to congratulate him for his unusual abstention from the brand of cosmetic criticism that had been the hallmark of Revere reviews for several years. After his last lapse, George was back on the greasepaint wagon; the period of withdrawal was difficult, but rewarding. On the other hand, the Idea may have come when he found two tickets to a Broadway opening on his desk with a note from the chief drama critic: "The idea of *Othello* restaged to take place in the American army revolts me—thought you might be interested in seeing how they do Shakespeare uptown. You can have my lead box." Or, again, the Idea may have come from Ross, who, discouraged at George's unabated antagonism, growled, "Why don't you advertise for her, for Christ's sake?"

Regardless of its origin, the Idea grew swiftly, turning phototropically toward the evening's performance as a source of nourishment. George stood on the corner of Eighty-sixth and Third waiting for his crosstown bus to bring him home. Generally, during the summer, he would prefer the mile hike across the Park, but since Ross's article had appeared, he had stayed away from that area; he was afraid that he had become *persona non grata* with Freddy and his friends, and he did not wish to run into any of them by chance. It was a brightly limpid day, and George could see for what appeared to be miles up and down the broad avenue, lined with graph-paper precision by new office buildings, apartments, and skeletons of office buildings and apartments. As he waited for the bus to make its lonely way up from East River, he kept polishing the opening of his review for that night. It was a review that would be blocked out with care before the show and would contain probably the most important paragraph he would write for a long time.

The bus finally came, and George returned to his lead paragraph as the vehicle slid away from the curb and began its halting, erratic progress crosstown. The Idea had now become crystal clear in his mind. It resolved itself pellucidly into a comprehensive set of postulates, although it had been arrived at in a much more haphazard and unorganized way. An idealization of George's reasoning might look something like this:

A. There was little better than no chance that he would find Lynn by his current manner of search. This was becoming rapidly self-evident.

B. It was hardly likely that Lynn would return to him, as he had, within the space of two weeks, grievously insulted her and, apparently, tried to turn her and her mother over to the *Polizei*.

C. Yet, she loved him. (Needless to say, this was

a completely necessary speculation on George's part. It pleased him.)

D. Granted that this definition of the two worlds he was trying to bridge was correct and granted that his assumption about Lynn's feelings was reasonably accurate, what communication links remained open between them?

E. *Answer:* One and only one. If George were Lynn (a most unlikely conjecture, and one that would have rendered most of this story, in its present form, superfluous), would he not avidly read any article that appeared in the New York *Alarum* under the dear, darling, cherished byline "George Revere"? Of course he would. Therefore, she would. Ergo, he was going to have to insert a personal notice into the *Othello* review tonight that would be for Lynn's eyes, and Lynn's eyes only.

Unfortunately, it was not as easy as it might sound. It was extremely unlikely that Conklin would pass a drama review that started out, "Would the lovely young lady with whom the undersigned reviewer lived in Central Park please contact the *Alarum* office, as he still loves her." It was also extremely unlikely that George Revere would ever enter the doors to the Alarum Building again if he tried it. This was the puzzle that George was working on as his bus disgorged him a block from his apartment, and he proceeded slowly home under a flickering light bulb labeled "THINK."

That light bulb was still flickering uncertainly, and had been joined by a balloon containing a log of wood and a saw, labeled "z-z-z-z," as the performance of *Othello* ground to a close. It was so quiet you could hear an option drop.

"To you, lord governor, remains the censure of this hellish villain," Major Lewis of the United States Army was saying to the head of the American Military Government in Germany, "the time, the place of torture." He looked with what passed for hatred at his acting

school in the direction of Lieutenant Colonel O'Malley.
O'Malley, held by two MP's, was clutching his wounded
arm and staring expressionlessly across the corpses piled
on the stage, one of which was his recently late superior, Major General Joe Thellow, an upright Negro
combat officer. The place, Frankfurt. The time, 1946.
The play, lousy.

"O enforce it!" Lewis went on. "Myself will straight
aboard, and to the state this heavy act with heavy heart
relate." All the live participants struck a tableau pose,
and the curtain came down.

"Come on," George hissed to Ginny, the amiable
redhead who was television's Miss Drainola and whose
favorite sport was playing musical beds. "Let's get out
of this mausoleum before lightning strikes."

Ginny didn't have the faintest idea what he was talking about but complied readily, a tactic that had ob-
tained the Miss Drainola title for her, and one that
would shortly make her the Playmate of the Month.
When the influence of her mother had receded, it had
been replaced by that of a shrewd agent: Ginny had
been too successful to attempt to do any thinking of her
own. For this reason, she did not fully realize what was
happening until she found herself sitting alone in a taxi
as George leaned in the window and gave the driver
instructions.

"Take the lady home. Here, this should cover it.
Good night, darling. See you around."

"Hey," said Ginny. It was an inadequate comment
under the circumstances, but it was all she could think
of. An invitation to see the opening of a Broadway
show had never before expired with the final curtain.
She always took it to include the subsequent night and,
at times, morning.

"Hey," she tried again, flinging open the door of the
cab. The exclamation caught the attention of a few
hardy theatergoers who were filing out of the audito-
rium; several of the men stopped short to watch Ginny's
legs and most of her thighs inch out of the open cab

door, followed an interesting moment later by the angry remainder.

"It's OK, Ginny," George tried to explain with what he hoped would pass for a lighthearted chuckle. "I've really got a lot of work to do."

"All night?" whined Ginny unbelievingly.

"Yeah, mister. All night?" came an echo from the crowd, followed by a soft patter of amusement like a television laugh track. George turned red.

"Look, Ginny. Be a good girl and get back in the cab and go home. I like you, but I've really got to get back to the office."

"The office!" a woman behind George said. "Imagine that!" "The poor girl," he thought he heard someone else say. He whirled around. "Yes, the office!" he snapped to the startled woman, and then turned back to Ginny. "OK, the fun's over. I've got to get to work. That's all in one-syllable words. Now, I had a marvelous time so far, so don't spoil it. Good night and pleasant dreams. I'll kiss you on the cheek if you want."

There was another round of light applause from the crowd, and George decided to take advantage of their favorable mood. He quickly bundled the protesting Ginny back into the cab and slammed the door.

"But what am I gonna tell my roommate? I mean, coming home so early and all," wailed Ginny.

"Tell her the play was so bad I had a nervous breakdown," said George. "Hey," called Ginny for the last time, but it was too late. The cab whirled her away into the maelstrom of Eighth Avenue, and George headed determinedly back to his office in order to face the challenging task of composition ahead.

Three drafts, two hours, and a dozen cups of coffee later, this is what he had:

There are those who say that shortly after the opening of *Othello* last night at the Julian L'Estrange Theatre, the late Mr. William Shakespeare revved up and began to spin like a gyroscope. Although this would appear to be physically unlikely, I intend to be at Madame Olga's Monday morning at ten o'clock to see, through her crystal ball, into the exact nature of Old Will's rotation. Any other gypsies who would be interested in exploring, with me, this scientific inquiry into the effect of theatrical oders on dead writers are encouraged to join me on East Sixty-second Street for the séance. If it should be discovered that the Bard had continued his quiet and peaceful sleep, I will bet an autographed photograph of Sir Henry Irving that he had merely been unaware of last night's production. It is my considered conclusion, however, that we will find the old boy dizzy as hell.

George read the paragraph over and over again. He felt that it had been laid on a trifle too thickly; the possibility that Conklin would run a blue pencil through it would not be overlooked. Hopefully, George doubted it. He thought it might go.

Pete stuck his head in the door. "Review will have to be set in half an hour, Mr. Revere."

George smiled for the first time in several weeks. "You shall have it, Peter. The forms will be locked up on time tonight." He inserted another sheet of paper in the old typewriter and continued, in fine form:

The idea of playing *Othello* in a setting provided by the American Military Government in Germany sounds like one of those brainstorms hatched up by inebriated ex-college-humor-magazine writers on Alumni Day; the handful of people who stayed to the final butchery testified more, I think, to the fascination of horror than to the enjoyment of delight. In my own case, I have to plead sleep—a deep sleep that lasted most of the final act and served admirably to knit up the ravel'd sleave of mutilation. . . .

"Jeez, you're a sarcastic bastard," said Conklin disapprovingly the next day. " 'The ravel'd sleave of mutilation' is a bit much, but I let it go. But what the hell was the classified ad in the first paragraph? What kind of payola do you get from Olga—fortune cookies?"

George's pulse livened noticeably; he replied, "Just thought it was good for some laughs."

"If I need laughs, I'll hire Danny Kaye," said Conklin. "All I want is good feature writing, including reviews. I let it go, too, because I like the way you write. One of these days, though, if you keep up this snotty bit, it's gonna mean a heave-ho, Revere. You're only about three uppity pills away from *The New Yorker* now."

"Hell, it was a lousy show," protested George. "What do you want me to do? Say it was the greatest thing since chastity belts?"

"All right, all right," said Conklin. "I give up. But just remember, try to stay away from the more obvious plugs. One more Madame Olga, and you'll be back running copy downstairs."

"Yes, sir," said George, saluting. "Hopefully, I've used all the Madame Olgas I'll need."

14 How Madame Olga Listened and George Heard a Knock

"It's a hard thing to cancel yourself out when you have to—especially in a city like New York. You understand—when you're surrounded day after day by millions of people who don't give a damn for you—and shouldn't—and for whom *you* don't give a damn—and shouldn't—you tend to drift more and more into yourself as the center of this world. It's like a Mixmaster whipping cream: the longer you stay in that whirlpool at the center, the thicker and thicker your shell becomes, until it becomes almost impossible, anymore, to make any kind of true contact with the outside."

George sat in Madame Olga's sunlit store. It was 10:15 the following Monday; he had kept up his end of the Idea. Madame Olga faced him across a checkered tablecloth; she wore a simple, colorful shirtwaist dress, with only a comparatively light scattering of bead necklaces, considering her profession. She was patient and attentive; her hands played incessantly with a pack of cards, shuffling and reshuffling them into endless combinations.

"You forget the idea of love so quickly," George went on. "It gets farther and farther away as the whipped cream gets thicker; pretty soon there's not a chance than anyone will be any more than a brief interest—a flashing affair. That becomes the end rather than the means. You're building up to nothing, after a while—just building up. Unless someone moves in and gets caught up in your whirling mess. You've seen what happens then: it's like the more modern mixers, with two blades instead of one. The two little whirlpools overlap in the middle, but they never get any closer, never get any farther apart. And then they, too, harden and disappear. That's what happens to love in New York: it can become a permanent liaison, continuing on momentum and never heading anywhere. That's where I was, without knowing it, when I met her."

The art of telling a good story is a consummate one. It is held by an extremely small number of blessed individuals who are or who have been; only the merest handful of these have ever put pen, or typewriter type, to paper. On the other hand, the unfolding of the truth is no art; it is a talent which everyone possesses, which anyone can use. George had put in long and serious hours of thought about himself for the first and, he hoped, the last time in his life. Because he was reasonably intelligent, he had saved himself the expense of a psychiatrist. Because he had an Event to illuminate his problems, like a lighthouse on a reef, he was able to reach certain conclusions. In Madame Olga's quietly solicitous presence, he found he could describe these conclusions in a way he had never been completely able to describe them to himself. As they were the truth, he found he could do it very well.

They sat at a small table, curiously together in the empty room. George stared at the ashtray in front of him, in which he had already stubbed out three cigarettes and in which the fourth was burning itself slowly down. He spoke quietly and insistently; he knew exactly what he wanted to say and had no trouble saying it. Madame Olga compulsively kept shuffling her pack of cards. She knew what was expected of her; she was a born listener, a trait that is the *sine qua non* of a great many trades, not the least of which is reading and advising.

"Of course," George continued, "if I hadn't sprung back into my little world so quickly, I would have brought her with me. It would have been fairly easy—at least, it's damn' easy to *say*—but I wasn't able to make the step. In one minute I was happy just to be happy, and in the next I was suddenly back to the long dull grind. There was nothing I could tell her, short of good-bye, so I blew up. That was the only way I could tell her that she had disrupted my life by making me aware of other people besides myself; I shouted at her like a petulant brat. And then, when that article appeared, I knew it was over. I had to go back and see, but I knew, deeply, that I had closed all the chinks in my armor and I was sealed into my life again—safely, inevitably, and finally."

A fly buzzed through the mail slot in the front door and began executing a series of glide approaches and Immelmann turns over their heads. Somehow the drowsy rise and fall of this raspy sound seemed to fit the warm atmosphere of sunlight, autumn, talking, and listening. The fly suddenly made a steep dive and dropped to the floor; it moved its feelers uncertainly for a moment and then headed for a curtain on the far wall, under which George had been watching a pair of red high-heeled shoes.

George had seen the shoes before the fly brought them into the picture again; he had been watching them off and on since he had entered Madame Olga's a half hour before. This is not to say that George had fetishist leanings—far from it. There was absolutely nothing out of the ordinary about this particular pair of shoes, except that they appeared to contain a pair of feet. The latter occurrence, George thought, made it a fit subject for observation. If Madame Olga had noticed George's preoccupation with the shoes, she gave no outward sign.

"You mean to say, dearie, that you had nothing to do with that story?" she asked.

"Nothing," said George emphatically. "That is, I know I'd been giving Ross bits and pieces of the whole account. Once in a while I would think of something funny or memorable, and if Ross was around I would tell it to him. I never dreamed that he would—"

George hesitated for a moment.

"Well, maybe I did. I knew I didn't want to, but maybe that's why I told the story to Ross. I could have been hoping that he might publish it. But I swear that when I first saw the story, the first thing I felt was hatred—both at myself and Ross. Then I was sorry, but it was too late."

"Boy, you both sure made a mountain out of a mole-hill."

"No, *I* made the mountain. For years and years I had been building that mountain, a bit at a time. I would never have met her if that mountain was as firm as I had been intending—I see now that I stopped building in time. I can never go back to my side, alone, again." George paused for a stray thought and watched the fly explore the toe of the left red shoe. "I don't know if I can really explain to you, Olga, what it's like to be separated from other people and other emotions by this mountain of routine and self-satisfaction. You probably move around pretty freely in your—ah—circle; I'm sure it's *alive*. This must all sound crazy and unnecessary to you."

"Not at all, dearie." Madame Olga, who owned (through an agent) four apartment buildings in The Bronx, had her own ideas about social mobility. "I just think it's a good thing that you know the score for yourself."

"That's the trouble. I know the score, as you said, but it's worse than if I didn't."

"How come?"

"Because I don't know when I'll ever see her again, and the score is, simply, that I must. A no-hit shutout against me. I can't stand up to that kind of a game the way I've been doing for the past ten, fifteen years." He was watching the shoes again, but they were motionless. The fly had disappeared as quickly as it had come, leaving a light buzzing on the fall air.

"Shall I cut the cards, dear?"

"No, don't bother." George looked at his wristwatch and then stood up abruptly. "My time is up, and I don't want to keep you. But if you see the girl I'm looking for in your cards, or in your crystal—tell her I think I know why she didn't trust me to stay the same afterward. Tell her she was right, but that the important thing is that I know she was right and I know why. That's really all."

He stood at the table uncertainly, as if he were waiting for something to happen. Madame Olga did not even look up, but continued her slow shuffle of the cards from one hand to another. A king of hearts floated gently to the floor; she barely watched it go. George stooped to retrieve it, placed it face up on the table, and left quickly.

The bells on the door jangled once, sharply. His shadow passed the curtained window and then disappeared. Madame Olga quietly dealt a queen of hearts, face up, next to the king.

As dusk settled slowly over the spires of Manhattan, obscuring first the Empire State Building's web of television antennae and then falling to blanket the aluminum lance of the Chrysler Building, other people besides George were caught up in the same metronomic beat with which time inched the day along.

Mr. Hamilton Elincar was seated at a workbench in the basement of his home in Brooklyn. Strange metal cases sprouting wires in many colors and sizes were scattered across the table, as were several oddly shaped wrenches and pliers. He held a smoking soldering iron in his hand. Slowly he leaned over the chassis upon which he was working. One last short wire in this newer, more powerful radio jammer remained to be soldered into place. Carefully he grasped the wire to attach it to the correct tube; so intent was he on the completion of his *chef d'oeuvre* that it was only gradually brought to his shocked awareness that he had neglected to disconnect the power.

Sol Berman sat entranced in front of his television set; he was watching his favorite western, _Laramie Dragnet_. To be precise, he was watching a commercial, for _Laramie Dragnet_ was sponsored by Royal Purple Stamps; it was Berman's tribute to the country of his birth. "Americana," he said proudly to his wife, who never listened to him anyway, "that's what made this country great." He pressed a button on the remote-control switch to raise the volume.

> Royal Purple Stamps! Royal Purple Stamps!
> Lotsa cameras, lotsa lamps!
>
> Hear the New York shoppers buzz:
> "Purple is as Purple does!"

"Peace," sighed Berman. "It's wonderful."

Oliver was standing dejectedly at the corner of Fifth and Fifty-ninth, as he always had. He knew clearly that there would be nothing exciting in his equine future, but as he plunged his face into the cool water of the A.S.P.C.A. tank he could at least remember a wonderful night of dirt under his hooves, the touch of the riding crop, and the stirring cry of "Gidyap."

Mr. Cuttleworth was taking the garbage cans out for the evening. First, as was his custom, he had explored the cans thoroughly for salvage; he could never understand the mentality of tenants who would just as soon throw away a perfectly good cigar box as not. Tonight he had reclaimed a dish that was broken neatly in half (a little Duco would make it good as new) and a hat with a missing piece in the brim (So who uses a hatbrim anyway?). There were many rewarding moments in Mr. Cuttleworth's life; the hour of dusk, when he could ransack the garbage cans before putting them out, was one of them. As he hauled the last can up the cellar stairs, he heard the front door click open and footsteps in the hall. First came a heavy tread with a short scuffling noise at the end—that would be Flack on the fourth, with his elevator shoes. Immediately after, he heard a lighter, more hesitant step which was accompanied by the tell-tale ticking of a woman's heels. He rounded a bend at the halfway point in the basement stairs, just catching a glimpse of a pair of red high-heeled shoes starting the ascent toward the second floor. I *wonder whose she could be? Kluger on Three? Westerman on Five? His wife's away. Revere again?* Mr. Cuttleworth stopped, listening carefully to see where the ticking footsteps would stop.

George Revere sat hunched over his desk and picked bleakly at his fingernails. A cigarette filter was burning malodorously in the ashtray near his elbow. Outside the big bay window in the living room, West Eighty-seventh Street had darkened from white to gray-orange to aquamarine to royal blue to black—the spectrum of dusk on a city street. The sidewalk cries had diminished; the steady *bulip-buloop* of a rubber ball hurled incessantly at a stoop across the street had finally stopped.

Only one light burned in George's apartment: the desk lamp cast a sickly fluorescent glow over the corner of the room in which he sat. Darkness had fallen quickly in this land of endless canyons, where the horizon is a neighbor's roof. Darkness had entered the apartment even more quickly, and George, thinking deeply and quietly about things in general, had not yet risen to turn on any other lights.

The calmness of the early evening was reassuring, as if it boded peace not only to the night but also to himself. Occasional sounds would drift up to him—an automobile horn on Central Park West, some footsteps on the stairs, Mr. Cuttleworth wrestling with the garbage cans. These sounds only added to the feeling of permanence and increased his reassurance. Can tragedy really lurk in a warm, friendly Manhattan apartment while the twinkling lights of evening guard its windows?

George sat motionlessly, tuning himself to his own time and his own sounds as the hands of the clock on the mantel inched forward. Finally he moved slightly, reaching into the center drawer of his desk and bringing out the little square of notepaper he had rescued from his wastebasket. He laid it carefully on the blotter in front of him. The seven hastily scrawled words stared up at him; if they had become wearied by his repeated readings during the past few days, they did not show it. Instead, to George, at least, each loop, curve, and dotted *i* retained a freshness and a promise that added two hundred watts to the light on his desk.

He studied this luminous inscription for a few moments, one inevitable refrain overwhelming any other thoughts: *I would I could make thee believe I love.*

All at once he was no longer listening to the small sounds of night, but to a specific noise that sent him bounding off his seat as if he had been grievously wounded by a misplaced thumbtack. The light tapping on his door could barely be classified as a knock, although it was firm and measured enough to send a thrill of recognition along George's spinal cord. *Dum, dee, dee—*

He had the door open before the familiar rhythm was half completed. The pair of red high-heeled shoes that stood on his threshold were filled, engagingly, by a familiar pair of lovely feet. This time, however, the feet supported, visibly, a pair of good sturdy legs, upon which . . .

"This must be the place," said Lynn, her hand still raised midway in the interrupted knock.

"Yes," said George, as the elusive feeling of tranquil happiness for which he had been waiting spread, like a quilt, over New York City and (for all he knew) the world, "this is the place."

Epilogue

If you happen one day to be traveling down U.S. Highway 20 in the state of New York, you will eventually pass through the county of Appalachia, set like a painting into the emerald-green rolling foothills of the Adirondack Mountains. (If you are truly curious, you will almost certainly be traveling by this particular route, which parallels the knife-slash of the Thruway and which is the only civilized way to travel through New York, except on foot.)

Just past the county seat, you can turn off 20 onto a wavy macadam road that cuts irregularly south into a region of tall elm trees and small still ponds. The macadam will soon give out (there is a proposition up for consideration in the town board which would continue it as far as Pine Ridge, but the residents have turned the bill down before and they are expected to turn it down again), and the road becomes two worn tire tracks in the dirt. As you proceed down this path—called a connecting road in the euphemistic terminology of the Esso map—you will hear the sound of weeds scraping against your automobile's underside and rocks being scattered by your wheels. You are now on Rural Free Delivery Route 4 and about a quarter of a mile from the rambling frame farmhouse in which the Appalachia *Gazette* is published weekly by George Revere and his wife.

Their farm is not big in size; seven acres of top-grade soil, never sprayed (Freddy was emphatic on that point), can produce enough for a great many more than the five people who, at present, inhabit it. And its mod-

est price—put together with George's savings, the one
thousand dollars Freddy had won in his friend's lottery,
and a minuscule GI mortgage—had even provided a
pond for Hortense.

The *Gazette* is a conservative paper, but then conser-
vation is a major issue outside of all city limits, and
George's paper scrupulously handles no news more distant than the county line. It is for mother, topsoil, and
rain; against Dutch elm blight, subdivision, and de-
creases in soil-bank payments. George produces it himself on an old flat-bed printing press in the barn; Lynn
takes care of the typing, proofreading, and subscription
lists.

For a country paper, the *Gazette* abounds in features.
Sally Harmony runs an astrology column which has become so popular that the general store has begun to
stock tarot cards and zodiac charts. Freddy contributes
an occasional piece about the merits of organic farming;
he has turned their seven acres into a shining example
of the virtues of mulch, manure, and individualism. All
of this is published with charming line drawings by El
Greco, who acts as lithographic consultant to the editor
and publisher when he is not tending the art museum.

The *Gazette's* art museum is, of course, one of the
centers of culture in the county; more people visit it every year, says the Appalachia Chamber of Commerce,
than visit Borkman's Cave and Balancing Rock com-
bined.

As official curator of the collection, El Greco has become a respected elder of the community. The people
who come to stare at the three Rembrandts, the Vermeer, the two Cézannes, the Lautrec, the two Goyas,
the three Millets, the two Holbeins, the four Corots, the
Monet, and the Whistler agree that the originals, which
Greco tells them are in the Metropolitan, couldn't be
any more beautiful. (The lone exception, a Pine Ridge
girl who had studied Art Appreciation at Wellesley, said
that they were rather poorly executed; George and
Lynn had to spend a week calming Greco down.)

But one young boy, who had been to the Metropolitan, told El Greco that the paintings in his museum were far lovelier than the originals, and that was good enough for everybody.

Share the strange adventures of an
orphaned boy after the Civil War!

The Fool Killer

HELEN EUSTIS

George woke up with a jump. More footsteps creaking
up the stairs. He knew it was Mr. Galt walkin' easy so's
not to wake anyone; but at the same time, with his heart
in his throat, he thought: *"That's the Fool Killer, eight
foot tall with his chopper in his hand, licking his lips
and his mouth watering. Come on!"* He said to him inside his head: *"Come on and get me! Looks like however I do is the wrong way anyhow!"*

"The book is nearly as prodigal of amazing characters as
one by Dickens and it rises to a climax as violent and
breathtaking as Stevenson could have devised."

—*San Francisco Chronicle*

A LAUREL-LEAF LIBRARY BOOK 95¢ 3197-07

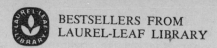

BESTSELLERS FROM
LAUREL-LEAF LIBRARY